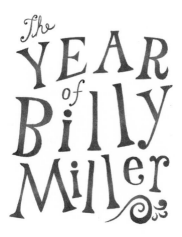

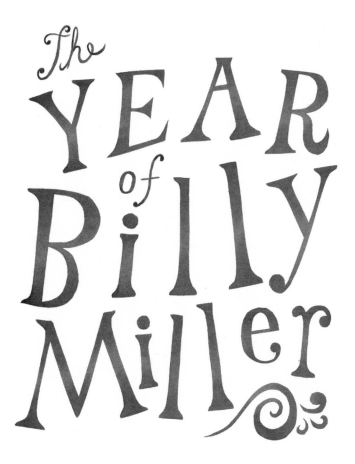

The YEAR of Billy Miller

Kevin Henkes

Greenwillow Books

An Imprint of HarperCollins*Publishers*

The Year of Billy Miller
Copyright © 2013 by Kevin Henkes

All rights reserved. No part of this book may be used or reproduced in any manner whatsoever without written permission except in the case of brief quotations embodied in critical articles and reviews. Printed in the United States of America. For information address HarperCollins Children's Books, a division of HarperCollins Publishers, 10 East 53rd Street, New York, NY 10022.
www.harpercollinschildrens.com

The text of this book is set in 13-point Century Schoolbook BT.
This book is printed on acid-free paper.
Book design by Kevin Henkes
Hand-lettered display type by Ryan O'Rourke

Library of Congress Cataloging-in-Publication Data

Henkes, Kevin.
The year of Billy Miller / by Kevin Henkes.
pages cm
"Greenwillow Books."
Summary: Seven-year-old Billy Miller starts second grade with a bump on his head and a lot of worries, but by the end of the year he has developed good relationships with his teacher, his little sister, and his parents and learned many important lessons.
ISBN 978-0-06-226812-9 (trade bdg.)—ISBN 978-0-06-226813-6 (lib. bdg.)
[1. Elementary school—Fiction. 2. Schools—Fiction.
3. Family life—Wisconsin—Fiction. 4. Humorous stories.] I. Title.
PZ7.H389Ye 2013 [Fic]—dc23 2012050373
13 14 15 16 CG/RRDH 10 9 8 7 6 5 4 3 2 1
First Edition

 Greenwillow Books

To Four—

Wife: Laura
Son: Will
Daughter: Clara
Teacher: Susan

Part 1: TEACHER

Part 2: FATHER

Part 3: SISTER

Part 4: MOTHER

PART ONE

TEACHER

1

It was the first day of second grade and Billy Miller was worried. He was worried that he wouldn't be smart enough for school this year.

There was a reason he was worried. Two weeks earlier on their drive home from visiting Mount Rushmore and the Black Hills of South Dakota, Billy Miller and his family stopped in Blue Earth, Minnesota, to see the statue of the Jolly Green Giant. Billy instantly recognized the Giant from the

1

labels of canned and frozen vegetables. The statue was spectacular—so tall, and the greenest green Billy had ever seen.

Billy was wearing his new baseball cap that said BLACK HILLS in glossy silver embroidery. It was a blustery day. The flag on the nearby pole snapped in the wind. Billy raced ahead of his family—up the steps to the lookout platform. As he stood between the Giant's enormous feet, a sudden gust lifted his cap from his head. His cap sailed away. Without thinking, Billy stepped onto the middle rung of the guardrail, leaned over, and reached as far as he could. He fell to the pavement below. The next thing Billy remembered was waking up in a hospital. His parents, whom he called Mama and Papa, were with him, as was his three-year-old sister, Sally, whom everyone called Sal.

After tests were done, the doctor proclaimed Billy miraculously unharmed, except for a lump on his head. "You fell exactly the right way to protect yourself," the doctor told him. "You're a lucky young man."

"And Papa got your hat back!" said Sal.

When they returned home, Billy proudly showed his lump—and his cap—to his best friend, Ned. He called his grandmother on the phone and told her about the incident,

3

too. Everything seemed all right until a few nights later when Billy overheard his parents talking in the kitchen.

"I'm worried about him," said Mama.

"He's fine," said Papa. "Everyone said he's fine. And he seems fine. He *is* fine."

"You're probably right," said Mama. "But I worry that down the line something will show up. He'll start forgetting things."

"He already forgets things," said Papa. "He's a seven-year-old boy."

"You know what I mean," said Mama. She paused. "Or he'll be confused at school. Or . . ."

That's all Billy heard. He snuck up to his room and closed the door. And that's when he started to worry.

Billy didn't tell anyone that he was worried. Sometimes, he didn't know how to say what he was thinking. He had words in his head, but they didn't always make it to his mouth. This happened often, even before the fall.

"Happy first day of school," said Mama.

"Happy first day of school," said Papa.

Billy had noticed long ago that one of his parents often repeated what the other said.

Without taking the time to sit at the table, Mama rushed about the kitchen, stealing a few bites of Papa's toast and a gulp of his coffee. She hoisted her big canvas bag onto the counter and reorganized its contents.

It was Mama's first day of school, too. She taught English at the high school down the street.

While Billy was eating his pancakes, Papa reread aloud the letter that Ms. Silver, the second grade teacher, had sent during the summer.

In the letter Ms. Silver greeted the students and said she was looking forward to the new school year. She said that she and her husband had a baby boy at home. And two dogs. She said that second grade would be "a safe, happy year of growth" and "a wonderful, joyful, exciting challenge."

Billy stopped chewing when he heard the word *challenge*. He put down his fork and touched the lump on his head. He didn't want a challenge.

Papa continued. "Ms. Silver says you'll be studying colors and habitats and the world of names."

"That sounds like fun," said Mama. "*My* students will be studying *Beowulf* and *Paradise Lost*."

"I'd rather be in second grade," said Papa, smiling.

Unlike the other fathers Billy knew, Papa stayed home and took care of Sal and the house. Papa was an artist. He was waiting for a breakthrough. That's what he always

7

said. He was currently working on big sculptures made of found objects. Pieces of old machines, tree limbs, and broken furniture filled the garage and spilled out onto the driveway. They were scattered across the yard, too. Billy loved watching Papa work. There was always something lying around that was fun to play with.

"Gotta go," said Mama. She kissed Papa on his bushy orange beard. She kissed Billy on his lump. "Have a fantastic day," she said. "And kiss Sal for me when she wakes up."

Just like that, Mama was gone, the smell of her lemony shampoo hanging in the air for a moment.

Papa cleared his throat and shook Ms. Silver's letter with a flourish. Billy could tell he was trying to be funny. In a deep, rumbly voice he said, "This utterly fascinating letter concludes by stating that currently this is, in fact, according to the Chinese, the Year of the Rabbit." Papa used his regular voice again. "That's pretty great, don't you think? The Year of the Rabbit."

Billy shrugged. Normally this would have interested him, but he was preoccupied.

"Maybe you'll have carrots for a snack every day," said Papa.

Silence.

"Papa?" said Billy.

"Hmm?"

"But, Papa, will I be smart enough for second grade?"

"Of course you will," said Papa. He was looking right at Billy, directly into his eyes.

Billy glanced down at what was left of his pancakes. With his thick, work-gnarled finger, Papa lifted Billy's chin. Their eyes met and held. "Ms. Silver and the great nation of China might think that this is the Year of the Rabbit," said Papa. "But I know—and I know everything—that this is the Year of Billy Miller."

Billy smiled. He couldn't not. He repeated Papa's words in his head. This is the Year of Billy Miller.

2

Billy was waiting by the front door. "I'm ready," he said.

Papa was waiting at the bottom of the stairs. "We're ready," he yelled up to Sal.

"I'm ready, too," Sal called back from the upstairs hallway. "It's the Drop Sisters who are slow this morning. They all have to go to the bathroom."

"Well, tell them to hurry up," said Papa. "We need to leave."

"Coming," said Sal. The toilet flushed. Then Sal descended the stairs dragging a grungy pillowcase behind her. The pillowcase was full and lumpy, and it bumped silently down each step. Inside the pillowcase were the five Drop Sisters: Raindrop, Dewdrop, Snowdrop, Gumdrop, and Lemondrop. They were nearly identical, pale yellow plush whales. Each had blue button eyes and water spouts made of glittery white yarn.

Raindrop was the original Drop Sister and was the most worn, the most  beloved. The others had been bought by Mama and Papa or given by relatives in case

Raindrop was ever lost. They'd been hidden in Mama and Papa's closet. One day Sal found them by accident and adopted them instantly.

"I think you're smarter after you go to the bathroom," said Sal.

"I didn't know that," said Papa. With his hand on her shoulder, he scooted Sal along. "We don't want to be late."

"I wish I could go to school," said Sal.

"You will," said Papa. "Soon enough."

"I wish I could go now," said Sal.

"I wish you could go for me," said Billy.

"Go, go, go," said Papa. "Everybody go."

And they—Billy, Papa, Sal, and the Drop Sisters—were off to Georgia O'Keeffe Elementary School in Constant, Wisconsin.

೧‘ೞ

Billy's best friend, Ned, was leaning against the stop sign at the corner. His mother, Amy, was standing beside him, fluffing his hair. She glanced at her watch.

"We're running a little late," said Papa, leading the way, nearing the corner. "Sorry."

"Hi, Lumpy," Ned said to Billy. He laughed. "Hi, Papa." He ignored Sal.

"My lump's almost gone," said Billy. He hoped that when the lump disappeared so, too, would his worrying.

"Don't call him Papa," said Sal. "He's not *your* papa. You should call him Cliff."

Ned paid no attention to Sal.

Ned always called Billy's father Papa.

Billy thought this was funny, but it bothered Sal. Ned called his own father Dad; everyone Billy knew called their own fathers Dad. When he was little, Ned had thought that Papa was a name like Billy or Cliff or Sal. Now he knew better, but it was a habit hard to break and a joke everyone but Sal enjoyed. Lately Billy had considered calling Papa "Dad" in public. He wondered if the word *Papa* sounded babyish. It was one thing for Ned to use it for fun, but another thing for Billy to use it for real.

"I can't believe you two are second graders," said Amy.

"I can't believe you're walking us to school," said Ned.

"Just today," said Amy. "Give your poor mother a little joy."

"And we'll stay a safe distance behind you," said Papa. "We won't embarrass you."

It was only five short blocks to school. Billy and Ned walked as fast as they could, to get away from their parents. Walking fast made something click inside Billy. He felt as if he had a motor embedded in his chest, independent of his control. The motor was revving up. "Let's run," he said.

After several long strides, Billy heard the joyful, rowdy sounds of his schoolmates, and was drawn to them as if he were being pulled by a strong invisible force. When they reached the edge of the playground, Billy turned around. Papa, Sal, and Amy were more than a block away. He and Ned waved good-bye and then plunged into a noisy group of kids charging around the playground like a pack of dogs.

The bell rang much too soon for Billy. Everyone lined up along the fence by grade. Mr. Tuttle, the principal, kept saying, "Welcome back!" with a megaphone. Billy and Ned pretended they held megaphones and yelled, "Welcome back to you!"

And then, at Mr. Tuttle's command, Billy's line moved. Caught up in the motion, he was pushed and pulled until he found himself funneled into the old brick building and entering Room 2.

3

Ms. Silver had chopsticks in her hair. That was the first thing Billy noticed about her. Her wavy blond hair was coiled into a bun and held in place with two shiny  red chopsticks. Billy's parents liked to eat with chopsticks sometimes, but he had never seen chopsticks on someone's head before.

Without thinking, Billy whispered, "Chop, chop" as he filed past her. Ms. Silver just smiled at him, but then, she seemed to be smiling at everyone, even Ned who asked, "How many days of school until summer vacation?"

There were six tables with four chairs each arranged around the room. "Look for the place with your name," said Ms. Silver. "When you find your place, you may sit down."

"Here's my seat," said Ned. He pulled out his chair and plopped onto it. Then he patted the tabletop next to him. "Sit here," he told Billy.

It made sense that he would be next to Ned. After all, they were neighbors and best friends. Maybe Ms. Silver knew that they were friends. Billy sat down without looking at the name tag at his place.

Billy felt breath on the top of his head. He turned around. Standing too close was a girl he didn't recognize. Her eyes were narrowed to slits, her arms were crossed, and her fingers were drumming on her elbows at a rapid-fire pace.

"Excuse me," she said. "You're sitting at my place." She paused. "Unless *your* name is Emma Sparks, too. Then we have a problem."

The girl stepped aside to let Billy get up. "If your name is Billy Miller, you sit there," she said, pointing. "If your name is Grace Cotter, you sit there." She pointed again. "He must be Ned Henderson," she continued, nodding.

And then she pointed once more, this time at Billy. "I have a feeling you're Billy Miller."

Everything about the girl made it seem to Billy that she should be, at least, a third grader. She talked like an adult. She walked like an adult. And she wore her sweater tied around her waist, which for some reason seemed very adult.

Billy shuffled around the table to his spot, kitty-corner from Ned.

Grace Cotter slipped into her chair. Billy had known Grace since kindergarten. She was so shy she seemed almost invisible. Like vacuums, her wide eyes were sucking in everything.

When the four of them had settled into

their proper places, Emma Sparks smiled an enormous smile. "My nickname's Emster," she told them. "You can call me Emster."

Billy misheard her. "*Ham*ster?" he said in a voice much too loud. "Your name is *Ham*ster?"

Everyone laughed. The laughter was pleasing to Billy. It gave him a tingle. Whispers of "Hamster" rippled throughout the classroom.

Emma glared at him. "I said *Em*ster. E-M-S-T-E-R."

All of a sudden, there was a noise like a single, penetrating toll of a bell. The laughter quieted. Silence, except for the resonant sound.

Ms. Silver stood at the front of the

room beside her desk holding a little padded hammer. There was a small bronze gong at the corner of the desk. "Thank you," she said in a hushed tone. "Whenever you hear the gong, it means I'd like your attention."

Billy had never known a teacher with a gong. It had worked like magic—the room was noiseless, still.

Ms. Silver talked about herself for a while, and Billy's mind wandered. The next thing he knew, Ned was kicking him under the table. "Say your name and something about yourself," Ned whispered.

"I'm Billy Miller," Billy said. "And I—"

He couldn't think of anything to say. "I'm in second grade."

There were giggles. But the students weren't giggling *at* Billy. They were giggling because they thought what he'd said was funny. A good, warm feeling came over him.

But not everyone thought he was funny. Emma looked at him, rolled her eyes, and said, "You are so dumb."

The good, warm feeling vanished.

Later, when the students were writing and drawing in their new journals, Emma said to Billy, "Maybe you should write that you're in second grade so you don't forget."

Billy took two red markers from the

bin in the middle of the table. Using both hands, he held up the markers on his head as if they were the fiery horns of a devil. Then he stared at Emma with the meanest expression he could manage.

Ms. Silver happened to be walking by just then. She stopped and looked at Billy for a long moment.

Billy froze for a few seconds, then lowered his hands and dropped the markers back into the bin.

Ms. Silver raised one of her hands to her chopsticks. She frowned. Then she smoothed her hair and walked away. "Keep working, everyone," she said.

"Oh no," Billy whispered. It dawned on

him. Ms. Silver thought he was making fun of *her*. She thought that the two red markers were meant to be her two red chopsticks. She thought that the ugly face he'd made at Emma was an imitation of her, Ms. Silver.

Billy didn't know what to do. What he wanted to do was to run and run and run around the playground. Running always made him feel better. But he couldn't do that, so, in his journal, he drew a picture of a hamster and wrote: *Hamsters smell bad.*

4

Sal and the Drop Sisters were sitting in a row on the front porch steps. "I'm waiting for you," Sal called to Billy as he turned into the yard.

"Well, here I am," said Billy. "You can stop waiting."

Papa came around the house from the garage carrying a battered cello with only two strings. "Hi, Billy," he said.

"Hi, Papa."

"How was school?" asked Papa.

"Okay," said Billy.

"What did you do?"

"Nothing."

"Give me one highlight from your day," said Papa.

Billy was used to Papa's probing, although he didn't particularly like it. "There's a kid named Hamster in my class," he said.

"Boy or girl?" asked Papa.

"Girl."

"Maybe her parents are celebrities," said Papa. "They often give their kids unusual names."

"Huh?" said Billy.

"Nothing," said Papa. "How is Ms. Silver?"

Billy shrugged. An image of Ms. Silver's disappointed face rose up in his mind. He did not want to talk about her, although he knew his father would think that her chopsticks were very interesting. "Can we not have any more questions?" asked Billy.

"No more questions," said Papa.

Sal, who had been unusually silent, stood with her hands on her hips, and said, "Your school doesn't sound very fun. My school with Papa was more fun. Look what I can do."

Sal bent over and grabbed a book from a stack on the porch. "I can read Mama's favorite book," she said. She held up a worn paperback copy of *Pride and Prejudice*.

"You can't read that book," said Billy.

The book was definitely for adults.

"Yes, I can," said Sal. "Watch. I know the words *a* and *I*." She opened the book to the first chapter. Her finger scanned across the lines and down the page. "A . . . a . . . a . . . a . . ." She paused. "There's an I!" She flipped the page. Now her finger darted around. "A . . . I . . . a . . . a . . ." She slapped the book shut and beamed. "That was just two pages, but I can even read in the hundreds." She opened the book again, this time to page 223. "See," she said. "I . . . I . . . a . . ."

"That's not really reading," said Billy.

"Is so," said Sal. "*A* is a word and *I* is

a word." She looked to Papa.

"Well," said Papa. "It *is* reading. In a way." He wiggled his eyebrows at Billy. He was still holding the dilapidated cello. He plucked one of the two strings, making a dull, heavy sound. "And this is making music." He plucked again. "In a way."

Billy laughed.

"I found the cello today, among other treasures. Come to the garage. I'll show you."

"Me, too," said Sal. She gathered the Drop Sisters into her pillowcase. "I'm going to teach the girls to read," Sal told Billy. "I'm teaching Raindrop first. She's the smartest."

Billy followed Papa, and Sal followed Billy into the garage.

Papa's treasures for the day included: the cello, an old-fashioned telephone with a dial and a long curly cord, a gnarled piece of driftwood that looked like an elephant, and a shiny silver garden ball on a cement pedestal.

"We went to the dump," said Sal.

Billy realized that if he'd spent the day with Papa, he would have had more fun than he did at school.

"Does any of this speak to you?" Papa asked. He rotated the driftwood in his hands, eyeing it critically. "Any ideas how your old Papa can turn these lovely bits of rummage into art?" He placed the driftwood at his feet, then rubbed

the silver garden ornament as if it were a crystal ball. "Let's look into the future . . ." said Papa.

Billy and Sal leaned closer.

"What do you see?" Papa asked, joking, stroking his beard.

Billy didn't see the future, but if he could have, he would have liked to see Emma move to a different table at school, and he would have liked Ms. Silver to let him know, somehow, that she wasn't mad at him.

"I see me!" said Sal. She touched her nose to the silver globe, then drew her face back a bit. She repeated this movement several times, mesmerized by her distorted reflection. "I like the silver ball best," she said before she kissed her reflection.

"I like the telephone best," said Billy. But he didn't have any suggestions for how Papa could turn it into art. "It would be fun to take it apart." He was fascinated by seeing the internal works of things—the wires and gears and nuts and bolts.

"You should like the silver ball best," Sal told Billy. "It's silver just like Ms. Silver. You should give it to her. Then *you* would be *her* favorite."

Billy didn't care about being Ms. Silver's favorite, but he *did* care that she thought he'd been rude to her. Billy offered no response to Sal's comments, but because of them, he experienced the first flicker of an idea, an idea of how to make things right with Ms. Silver.

Ned came over, and he and Billy took apart the telephone with Papa's help.

And Billy's idea was forming.

Mama came home, and she asked even more questions about second grade than Papa had. Billy's answers stayed nearly the same: "Okay" and "Nothing" and "I don't know."

Billy's idea continued to form during dinner and throughout the evening. By the time he went to bed, he had a plan.

5

Before school, Billy gathered the following: a nickel, a dime, a quarter, a paper clip, a safety pin, and a nail. Each of these things was silver in color and each would be a gift for Ms. Silver. Billy wanted one thing more, something better somehow, something important, to add to his collection. When he was sitting on the edge of his bed putting on his shoes, he found it.

On his desk, beside his rubber band ball

and his gold soccer trophies, were his three silver animals—a bear, a dog, and a rabbit. The animals had been Mama's when she was a girl and they'd been on Billy's desk for as long as he could remember. The rabbit will be perfect, he thought, recalling  that Ms. Silver had noted in her letter that this was the Year of the Rabbit. He picked it up, turned the little thing in his hand. It was only an inch and a half high. Billy shoved the rabbit into his pocket with his other silver things.

His plan was to leave the silver items on Ms. Silver's desk. The gifts would be a way to show her that he was a nice person. He didn't think he could find the words to explain to her what he'd been doing with the red markers. He hoped this gesture would take care of the situation.

"Ned's here!" called Papa.

Billy bounded downstairs.

It was a foggy morning. Sal was standing at the front window with Raindrop, gazing out at the murkiness that pressed against the house. "Oh well," she said matter-of-factly. "There's nowhere to go today. Everything's gone." She shrugged and walked away from the window. "We'll try again tomorrow."

"It's so cool out there," said Ned. He was just inside the door. "You can barely see."

"Now don't get lost," joked Papa. "And

have a good day," he added, lightly squeezing Billy's shoulder as he slipped past him.

Billy and Ned were out the door in a flash, but Billy took his first steps through the dense air as if he were walking on dangerous ground.

"Maybe we *will* get lost," said Ned with glee.

"Maybe we'll end up in Lake Michigan," said Billy.

They ended up at school. The first person Billy saw on the playground was Emma. Because it was so foggy, she was just a few feet away when she made her presence known. Her cheeks were flushed. Like the day before, her sweater was tied around her waist. She held the empty sleeves in her hands, twirling them. She came right up to Billy and Ned and said, "Don't forget—you're in second grade. That's the grade after first." Then she dropped her sleeves and ran away.

"Hamster on the loose!" yelled Billy. And he and Ned chased after Emma. But they didn't really know what they'd do if they caught her, so they changed course. Around and around the foggy playground they ran until it was time for class.

Billy couldn't concentrate on schoolwork. His mission filled his mind. He wondered when he should put the silver things on Ms. Silver's desk. And how would she know they were from him? Should he write a note that said "From

Billy Miller"? He hadn't worked that part out.

Ms. Silver had been talking about different habitats. While she talked, she pointed to posters on the bulletin board labeled THE OCEAN and THE RAIN FOREST and THE PRAIRIE. Then she talked about the different names for the specific places animals live, their homes. She mentioned nests and webs and caves and dens and burrows.

She crossed the room to the cabinet in the corner and came back to the center of the room with a nest. A robin's nest. She carried

the nest to each table, with both hands, low, so that everyone could see it.

When she came to Billy's table, she leaned forward and extended the nest across the tabletop as if she were offering a bowl of snacks. Billy's eyes went right to Ms. Silver's chopsticks, which were mere inches from him. Then he tried to catch her eye and smile at her, but she was focused on the nest.

Next the students were told to write or draw in their journals.

"Share your thoughts about habitats," said Ms. Silver. "Draw where you'd like to live if you were an animal."

"Under the sea," said Ned, reaching for the bin of markers. "I get the blue ones."

"A castle for me," said Emma. "With lots of pink towers."

"That's not a habitat," said Billy.

"It is if you're a royal mouse," said Emma.

Grace didn't say anything, but she began a pencil drawing of the most intricate, delicate web Billy had ever seen.

Billy picked up a black marker because he was in a black mood. He just sat, staring at the blank journal page.

"What are you doing?" said Emma.

"Nothing," said Billy.

"As usual," said Emma.

Billy gripped the marker fiercely and covered a page in his journal with black scribbles, leaving space at the top to write:

Inside of Cave. He added: *Bat Habitat,* after looking to the bulletin board to see how to spell habitat. He wasn't a great speller. But now he could add *habitat* to the list of words he knew how to spell. He realized that it was one of those words that was spelled exactly as it sounded, even though it was a big word.

When the bell rang signaling the start of morning recess, everyone but Billy sprang up and quickly formed a ragged line at the front of the classroom. Billy lagged behind. He pretended to look for something under his chair. He thought he could wait until everyone had left the room, then place the silver things on Ms. Silver's desk unnoticed.

"Come on," Ned called in a loud whisper.

Billy ignored Ned and scrambled around on the floor.

"Everyone—listen," said Ms. Silver. "Go to your locker if you need a jacket. Then you may go outside." She was moving toward Billy. "Do you need help?" she asked in a private voice.

"No." Billy scooted under the table. He stared at the tile floor. He didn't know what to do.

Ms. Silver must have seen Billy's journal, because she said, "Are you a bat? Is that your cave?" She pulled a chair aside. "Come out of your cave, bat."

Billy moved out from under the table and stood. He glanced around. It was only the two of them. He was alone in Room 2 with Ms. Silver. He wished he were home with Papa and Sal.

"Are you feeling okay?" asked Ms. Silver.

Billy tried to nod, but his head and neck felt glued in place.

"Is there anything you want to tell me?"

Billy wriggled his hand into his pocket and pulled out his silver things. The nail got caught and made a little rip in his pocket. His hand was clammy. "Here," he said. "These are silver like your name."

Ms. Silver took the items and held them in both hands the way she'd held the nest. "Are these for me?" she asked.

Billy inclined his head shyly and softened

his voice to a whisper. "I'm really a nice person," he said. He couldn't look at her, but he could feel her eyes upon him like a net. His heart was thrumming.

"I can tell you're a nice person," she said.

Billy sighed.

"A very nice person."

Billy felt great relief.

"Tell me about this rabbit," said Ms. Silver.

"It was my mama's when she was little," Billy began. "I thought you would like it because it's the Year of the Rabbit."

"Does your mama know you brought it to school?"

"Oh, it's okay," said Billy. "It's mine."

"I *do* like it, but I think you should keep the

rabbit," said Ms. Silver. "I think you should keep the coins, too. But I can always use a paper clip. And a safety pin. And I should probably keep the nail, too. I'm glad it didn't poke you."

"I think it tore my pants a little."

During their conversation, Billy's eyes would flit up at Ms. Silver, but when he spoke he cast them downward.

"Here you are," said Ms. Silver. She placed the coins and the rabbit in his hand. "And thank you."

When, after a brief silence, he had the courage to look at her, really look at her, he did so with a kind of curiosity at first. He saw her differently, somehow, and suddenly, unexpectedly, he found it natural and easy to ask, "Do you think I'm smart enough for second grade?"

"Oh, Billy. Absolutely. Yes." She paused. "Are you worried about something?"

He told her his story—about falling—and he showed her his lump.

"Your bump is nearly gone," said Ms. Silver.

"The doctor said when I fell I protected myself."

"Well, that was smart of you," said Ms. Silver in a voice that was clear and kind. "You *are* very smart."

Billy blinked, as if by doing so he could replay Ms. Silver's last remarks.

The doctor in Minnesota had said Billy was *lucky*. But Ms. Silver had just said that he was *smart*.

Smart.

That one word said in Ms. Silver's voice made him feel as if he were filled with helium like a balloon and might rise off the floor.

"If you go quickly, you'll still have some time for recess," said Ms. Silver. "And, thank you for my silver things."

"I like your chopsticks," Billy said over his shoulder as he hurried out of the room.

When he got outside, he couldn't believe it—the fog had lifted; the sun had burned through the damp air. Everything was bright. Sharper. He spotted Ned and some other kids in a cluster at the far end of the playground. He rushed toward them.

He couldn't help smiling, even as he ran. He doubted he'd tell anyone about his talk with Ms. Silver. There really was nothing to say—even to Mama and Papa.

"Hey, Ned!" he shouted. He said no more until he reached his friend, but his mind was sending off sparks.

It's only the second day of school, he thought happily, and my teacher said I was smart.

PART TWO

FATHER

1

Things were changing. The light was different. The trees throughout the neighborhood were turning. Every day it seemed the leaves were more colorful, as if someone had taken a paintbrush to them during the night. There was a cool edge in the air and, lately, an edge to Papa, too.

"Why is Papa so crabby?" Billy asked Mama one Sunday morning in October. They were in the kitchen with Sal, getting breakfast together. Cinnamon muffins were in the oven and a mixing bowl of eggs was on the counter ready to be scrambled. During the week Papa cooked, but on the weekends Mama took over.

"I think he's having a hard time with his work," said Mama.

"Is he still waiting for his breakthrough?" asked Billy.

"That's one way to put it," said Mama. "Yes."

"Will his breakthrough come soon?"

"I hope so," said Mama.

"What's a breakthrough?" asked Sal.

Mama's mouth hitched upward into an exaggerated expression that said, *I'm thinking of the best way to explain this.* "Well, he's waiting for things to click," she told Sal.

Sal looked at Mama as if she had replied in a foreign language.

Mama said, "He's waiting for his work to go well."

"Papa's got a lot of things that click in the garage," said Sal.

"Yes, he does," said Mama.

Billy rolled his eyes and tilted his head toward Mama. Sometimes when Sal misunderstood, he felt superior.

Mama smiled.

57

The timer rang.

"Muffins!" cried Sal.

"Listen," said Mama, "I'll start the eggs. Sal, you can help me. Billy, go to the garage and tell Papa it's time to eat."

Billy didn't want to disturb Papa if he was busy. He entered the garage quietly. He was careful not to knock over Papa's new acquisitions: dozens of wooden cigar boxes stacked tall near the door. "Papa? Breakfast is ready."

Papa was sitting on a stool with his back to Billy, staring at his latest creation. Papa twisted, turning his head toward Billy, but remained seated. "What do you think?" asked Papa.

Billy came closer. Papa pulled Billy onto his lap, bouncing him twice, and Billy could tell Papa was making an effort to be cheerful. "I like it," said Billy. "What is it?"

"Good question," Papa replied.

Before them stood the broken-down cello Papa had found at the dump. He'd attached four store-mannequin arms to the cello, two on each side.

"It looks like the cello is playing itself," said Billy.

Papa nodded thoughtfully.

"And it sort of reminds me of a spider," said Billy.

Papa nodded again. He scratched his beard, then twirled part of it into a point.

"Is it your breakthrough?" asked Billy.

Papa took in a deep breath and loudly sighed it out. "No," said Papa. "No, no, no." His voice sounded sharp. He lifted Billy off his lap.

"You could add a monster mask on top," said Billy, trying to be helpful. "It would be easy to find a good one with Halloween coming up."

"Whatever," said Papa, his voice still sharp. He slapped his thighs as he rose from his stool. Then he offered Billy an apologetic smile. "Let's eat," he said.

Papa was quiet during breakfast. When they were cleaning up afterward, Billy reminded him, "Don't forget, Ned's coming over to work on dioramas."

Papa had said he'd help Billy and Ned with their habitat projects.

"Would you rather I work with the boys?" Mama asked Papa.

"No," answered Papa. "I said I would do it." He watched something out the window before adding unconvincingly, "We'll have fun."

"I get to make a dirama, too," said Sal.

"Di-o-rama," corrected Billy.

"What kind of habitat are you going to make?" asked Mama.

"A cave," said Billy. "For bats. And Ned's going to do the sea. He likes sharks."

"I'll do the sea, too," Sal announced. "The Drop Sisters are from there. I'll get them and tell them!" She dashed out of the kitchen.

"She's something," said Mama.

"She's something," said Papa.

What, exactly, the something was, Billy couldn't say.

2

While Mama graded papers in the dining room, the kitchen became a diorama workshop. Mama had found three shoe boxes in her closet that she was willing to give up— one for Billy, one for Ned, and one for Sal. Billy had gotten scissors, crayons, markers, construction paper, tissue paper, tape, and glue from the basement. Papa had thrown together some odds and ends from the garage that he thought might prove useful. Ned had brought two plastic sharks and some sea-shells from a Florida vacation to use for his diorama. And Sal had asked Papa if she could please, please, please use glitter, which was kept in a secret hiding place out of her reach.

At first, Papa seemed jolly and had good suggestions to offer. He showed Billy how to replicate a cave by crumpling up a piece of gray construction paper, then smoothing it out and gluing it to the inside of the box. Because the paper was crisscrossed with folds and wrinkles, it really gave the shoe box the appearance of worn, silvery rock.

Billy worked diligently. He had a vision in his head of how his diorama should turn out. He wanted to make three or four bats hanging from the top of the cave, and he wanted to make one big bat with its wings spread to look as if it were flying.

Billy cut several bats out of black construction paper. He worked quickly. The sleeping, hanging bats were fairly easy to make. Essentially they were black ovals with tabs on one end. Billy folded the tabs and taped them to the inside top of the shoe box.

He had some difficulty with the flying bat. His hands couldn't get the scissors and the paper to do exactly what he wanted them to do. After a few failed attempts, Billy grew frustrated. He ripped up yet another lopsided bat and tossed it onto the floor, grunting.

"Hey," said Papa, "what's the problem?"

"Nothing."

"Really?"

No answer.

"Do you need some help?" asked Papa.

"No," said Billy. He wanted to do it on his own.

"Okay," said Papa. "Fine." The sharpness had returned to his voice.

Billy finally cut out a bat that was acceptable, but he couldn't figure out how to attach it to the box and also make it appear as if it were flying, suspended in air. "Now will you help me?" Billy asked Papa.

Papa nodded.

Billy explained his idea.

"We can do this," said Papa. He cut a strip

of heavy paper and
folded it many times
like an accordion. He
glued one end of the
strip to the bat, and the other to the inside
of the box. Papa held the glued ends firmly
for what seemed like forever. "You have to be
patient with glue," he said.

At last, Papa angled the shoe box so that the
opening faced Billy. "How's this?" asked Papa.

If Billy looked at the diorama straight on,
he couldn't see how the bat was fastened to
the box. It truly looked as if the bat hung in
the air.

"That's good!" said Billy.

"You're welcome," said Papa.

67

"Thank you," said Billy. He shook the diorama gently and the bat bounced.

"Careful," warned Papa. "It's pretty delicate."

To complete his cave, Billy chose some pebbles from Papa's assortment of things from the garage and glued them to the bottom of the box. He was proud of what he'd done.

Billy had been so focused on his own diorama, wrapped in a cocoon of concentration, that he hadn't paid much attention to Ned's or Sal's. When he finally checked them out, a sinking feeling took hold of him.

Papa had helped Ned make an ocean from different shades of blue tissue paper, which he'd crinkled and layered. And, because Ned had used real seashells and the store-bought sharks, his diorama looked professional. He'd

also made two streaks of blood trailing from the sharks' mouths with glitter glue—a perfect, gruesome finishing touch.

Sal's diorama looked great, too. Her ocean was messy—patches and globs of blue, green, and silver glitter—but Papa had made a big, beautiful replica of Raindrop out of yellow construction paper. It filled most of the shoe box.

In comparison, Billy felt that his project looked like it was made by a two-year-old.

Sal watched Billy scrutinize his diorama. "Mine's better," she said. "Ned's, too."

"Mine's dumb," Billy mumbled.

"No, it's not," said Papa.

"Mine's pretty," said Sal. She was radiant. She hugged her diorama, swaying. "Papa, can we make a dirama for all the Drop Sisters?"

"Di-o-rama!" said Billy.

"Not today," said Papa.

Ned giggled. "Hey, Billy, your big bat looks like a pair of flying underwear. Black, *dirty* underwear." He giggled again.

"Well," said Billy, "yours only looks good because you have store-bought sharks." Any positive feeling had been drained away. Billy turned toward Sal. "And yours only looks good because Papa did it. If he hadn't helped you, it would look like garbage."

"Hey!" said Papa sternly. "Enough." He brought his hand down hard onto the table.

Smack. Then silence.

Papa rarely raised his voice, so when he did, it felt as if something in the universe had shifted.

Sal broke the silence. "Papa, your beard is sparkly," she said.

"Glitter," said Ned.

"That's the least of my problems," said Papa.

"I'm never having a beard when I grow up," Billy said under his breath. He was mad at Papa. Billy blamed him for the way he felt.

Mama entered the kitchen. "What's going on in here?" she asked. She tucked her red marking pencil behind her ear, which made Billy think of Ms. Silver's chopsticks.

Papa whisked past Mama, tapping her on the shoulder. "Tag team," he said. "Your turn." He disappeared out the back door.

Mama scanned the room. The tabletop and floor were strewn with scraps and wads of construction paper and tissue paper. There was a dusting of glitter everywhere. "I can tell you've been working hard," she said.

"Are you going to make a dirama, too?" asked Sal.

Mama sighed. "No, honey," she said. "I'm going to help you all clean up."

3

Before he climbed into bed, Billy put his diorama on his desk. He tapped the diorama and watched his bat jiggle. As the day had worn on, Billy had grown more fond of his project. The illusion that his bat was hovering in midair was what gave him a small thrill and a little shot of pride. When Billy stared at his trembling bat, all the imperfections disappeared.

Mama usually said good night to Billy

first, while Papa tucked in Sal. Then Mama and Papa switched places, and Papa came to Billy's room.

Billy and Papa had the same exchange every night.

Papa: Good night, Billy.

Billy: Good night, Papa.

Papa: You're a good boy.

Billy: Thank you, Papa, yes I am.

Papa: I love you.

Billy: Love you, too.

Papa: Love you more.

Billy: Tie.

Papa: Tie.

But this night, after their routine, and after Papa had turned off the light and was closing the door, Billy said, "Papa?"

"Yes?"

"I was thinking about your breakthrough," said Billy.

Papa left the light off, but returned to Billy's bed and sat on the edge of it. Billy could feel Papa's weight drag down the corner of the mattress. The bed groaned.

"What were you thinking?" asked Papa.

"I was thinking that you're so good at dioramas, that you should make dioramas for your artwork."

There wasn't much light, most of which came from the hallway behind Papa, but Billy could tell that Papa was stroking his mustache, then twiddling with his beard.

Papa breathed audibly. "Hmm."

"You have all those wooden cigar boxes," said Billy. "They would be good for dioramas."

Quiet. So quiet. Billy tugged on his covers, trying to readjust them, but they were anchored by Papa, unmovable.

"Interesting idea," said Papa. He breathed audibly again. "Hmm, hmm, hmm."

Billy imagined Papa smiling.

Papa leaned toward Billy and pecked the top of his head. He rose from the bed. As he walked away, his big adult frame darkened the doorway. And then he was gone. But Billy could hear him humming. The sound was low and rumbly. Simple and tuneful. Not quite happy. But definitely not crabby.

ᘓ˙ᘔ

"Fairies were here!" cried Sal when Billy came down to breakfast the next morning. "Look!" She moved her head from side to side and up and down. She was squinting, her eyes like small black seeds.

Billy moved his head in a similar fashion, trying to see what Sal was so excited about. When he held his head in certain positions, he noticed tiny pricks of light on the floor and on the table where the sun was shining. "It's just glitter," said Billy. "From yesterday."

"Fairies," said Sal.

"Glitter," said Billy.

They both looked to Papa for confirmation.

"Well," said Papa, with a sly smile, "it's all

in the eye of the beholder. What's glitter to one person could be fairies to another." He winked at Billy.

"Papa," said Billy. But he didn't press him, because Papa seemed to be in such a good mood.

"I love glitter," said Sal. She twirled with joy, spinning out of the kitchen. "My dirama has glitter," she called. "I'll go get it."

Billy settled into his usual place at the table and began eating breakfast: a banana and a toaster waffle in a puddle of syrup. "Where's Mama?" he asked between mouthfuls.

"She went to school early," said Papa.

"Why?"

"To help a student."

Billy wondered if that student wasn't smart enough for Mama's class. He ate quickly. He couldn't wait to see what Ms. Silver thought of his flying bat. "I love syrup," he said, as if thinking aloud, echoing Sal's statement about glitter.

"I can tell," said Papa.

Billy wanted a spoon so he could get every drop of syrup. As he crossed the kitchen to the silverware drawer, he glanced out the doorway into the dining room. Sal was kneeling on a chair at the dining room table. She was holding her diorama over Billy's, shaking the loose glitter from hers into his.

"Stop!" yelled Billy. "What are you doing?" He rushed to Sal and snatched his diorama off the table. "You are so dumb! You dope!"

In a flash, Papa was beside them. "What's up?" asked Papa calmly.

"She ruined my diorama. There's glitter everywhere. It's sticking to my bats and it's all over my cave. It looks like a girl made it."

"I was just giving you fairies," said Sal.

The urge to hit or pinch Sal was overwhelming. With laser eyes, Billy stared right through his sister. Underneath Sal's dense, dark curls clipped with a panda barrette and her lacy pastel nightgown, Billy saw the enemy. Why couldn't he have had a brother instead?

"Here," said Papa. "Let me see it." He took the diorama from Billy.

Billy searched Papa's face. He wanted an indication that everything would be okay.

"Now you have fairies in your cave," said Sal. She ducked her head, but her voice was bright.

"Why don't we—" said Papa, but before he could say more, the doorbell rang.

"Ned's here," said Sal.

"Oh no," said Billy. "What am I going to do? I'll be late for school."

Still holding Billy's diorama, Papa flipped the latch on the front door with his elbow and shouldered open the door. He told Ned to go to school without Billy. "He'll be there soon," said Papa. The door snapped shut, then Papa smiled reassuringly down at

Billy. "Let's go to the kitchen," he said.

Papa positioned Billy's diorama over the garbage bin and gently tapped it. He inspected it and tapped again. Then he gave it a good hard slap.

"It's still *full* of glitter," said Billy, his voice desperate.

"Wait here," said Papa. "I have an idea."

After a minute or so, Papa reappeared in the kitchen with Mama's hair dryer. "Maybe this will do the trick."

Papa had Billy hold the diorama. Papa steadied the big flying bat with one hand and carefully aimed the hair dryer with the other. The hair dryer roared. One wing of the bat jittered wildly.

Billy watched Papa's every move intensely. "Don't hurt my bat," he said loudly, over the noise of the hair dryer.

"Don't worry," said Papa. He used the hair dryer a bit longer. Then he brushed aside a few flecks of glitter from the big bat with his finger. "There," he said. "That's better. At least your bat is glitter free."

"But you didn't get it all," said Billy. "There's still glitter all over my cave."

Papa turned his head and glanced upward. His eyes narrowed as if he were trying to read tiny instructions on the ceiling. Then his eyes widened. "For a great reason," said Papa.

"What?" said Billy, confused.

"Listen," said Papa. "Rocks are made up of minerals, and certain minerals make rocks sparkle. Some caves have calcite crystals or mica in them. They can make a cave look like it's decorated with jewels."

Billy crinkled his eyebrows together. "Really?" he said.

"Really," said Papa. "This actually makes it better, more authentic."

"How do you know so much?" asked Billy.

"I don't know as much as you think I do," said Papa.

That was hard for Billy to believe. *"Mica?"* he said.

"Mica," said Papa.

"You're so smart, you could be a teacher like Mama," observed Billy.

Papa laughed. "Thank you," he said. "Now, if we hurry, you won't be late. I'll drive you."

They worked in unison like one big machine. Papa scooped up Sal, secured her in her car seat, put the diorama in the front seat next to him, waited for Billy to get in the back next to Sal and buckle his seat belt, and started off to school.

The bell was ringing as they approached the playground. "We made it," said Papa. Within seconds, Billy was out of the car, cradling his diorama, pointed toward the river of students flowing into the building.

"And they lived happily ever after," said Papa through the open window, loud enough for Billy to hear.

Billy took a few quick steps and stopped. He had forgotten something. He turned around. Papa was waving good-bye, starting to pull away. "Thank you, Papa!" yelled Billy.

When he turned back to run into school, Emma was right there, like a shadow. *"Papa?"* she said.

Billy blushed.

"Papa?" she repeated. She rolled her eyes dramatically. "That is so babyish, I can hardly believe it."

Abruptly, she spun on her heel and marched

ahead, carrying her diorama as if it were a gift for the president.

Billy shifted his weight from one leg to the other for a long moment before moving forward.

So much for happily ever after.

One by one the students in Room 2 stood beside Ms. Silver's empty desk and presented their dioramas to the class.

When it was his turn, Billy shook his diorama to demonstrate how his bat could fly, and he described his habitat, explaining how he'd used glitter to look like mica. He didn't mention Sal or fairies. He tried to remember Papa's words. He said, "Mica sparkles like jewels. It is a mineral in caves. It's like glitter."

Billy had been looking down as he spoke, but when he had nothing else to say, he raised his eyes, connecting with Ms. Silver's. She was in the far corner of the room sitting casually on the window ledge, holding a clipboard.

Ms. Silver nodded approval, and Billy felt proud. He also felt a surge of relief when he was done. Back with his tablemates, he sank into his chair, loose and slack as a rag doll.

"The glitter was a nice touch, Billy," Ms. Silver said before she called Ned to take his turn.

Billy glowed.

"Was the big bat the *Papa* bat?" Emma whispered.

Billy pretended not to hear her. He wanted to *be* a bat. First, he'd bite Emma. Poison her. Possibly causing death. And then he'd fly away—tracing widening circles in the sky—to a place where there were no girls.

"How'd it go?" asked Papa.

"Good," said Billy.

"Just good?"

"Great," said Billy.

"Tell me everything," said Papa.

"Ms. Silver liked my diorama," said Billy.

"And?" Papa waited for more information.

Billy shrugged.

"What did she say?" asked Papa.

Billy shrugged again. He hiked his shoulders high and held them there for a long time before dropping them. He was thinking about something else. He was thinking that he'd like to ask Papa if he minded if he called him Dad from now on. "She liked the glitter," he finally said.

"That doesn't surprise me," Papa replied. He raised an eyebrow playfully. "Mica," he said.

"Mica," Billy repeated.

They were standing in the weedy grass halfway between the house and the garage. Billy had gone straight from school to the backyard without checking for Papa in the house because he'd heard music coming from the direction of the garage. Country music. That usually meant that Papa was working and that his work was going well.

Papa's shirt was rumpled and dirty and buttoned wrong. Sawdust flecked his beard like cookie crumbs. All good signs concerning Papa and his work.

Billy glanced around the yard. "Where's Sal?" he asked. He didn't see his sister anywhere. If he knew he had some time alone with Papa, he'd tell him that he wanted to call him Dad.

"She's sleeping," said Papa. "Look." He motioned for Billy to follow him. Papa walked to the garage and stopped at the open door. He pointed to the worn velvet armchair in the corner. Sal was curled up in it like a cat, with her arms and hands pulled underneath her. Her head was resting on her lumpy pillowcase stuffed with the Drop Sisters.

"Isn't she cute?" whispered Papa. "Just looking at her shreds my heart."

Papa often said that things shredded his heart. Billy didn't quite understand what this meant, but Papa used the phrase when he talked about things Billy thought were sappy.

Billy edged silently away from the garage. He didn't want to wake Sal, although the country music coming from Papa's old paint-splattered radio seemed loud enough to mask any noise Billy might make.

"Do you want a snack?" asked Papa. "I baked cookies earlier."

Billy nodded.

They crossed the yard to the back door, and Billy tried to keep up with Papa, matching him stride for stride, stretching his legs with all his might.

At the kitchen table, with a plate of Papa's oatmeal raisin cookies between them,  and one cookie already in his belly, Billy asked his question. "Papa," he said, "can I call you Dad?"

Papa studied Billy for a moment. "No more Papa?"

Billy didn't know what to say. He didn't want to hurt Papa's feelings. "Well—" he began. "I'm in second grade now. Nobody says *Papa*." His voice clouded. "It's babyish."

Papa reached for his beard, tugged on it. "No more Papa." He made a sad face—a long, droopy, clown face—but Billy knew he was joking.

"Is it okay?" asked Billy.

"Of course," said Papa, smiling. He arched his eyebrows. "Maybe one day *you'll* want to be called something else."

Billy tilted his head. "Huh?"

"Maybe one day you'll want us to call you Bill. Or William."

"*No*," said Billy. "I'm Billy. Promise to always call me Billy."

Papa tugged on his beard again. "I promise to always call you what you want to be called."

"Billy," said Billy.

"Billy," Papa repeated. Then after a few seconds he said, "Hey, what about Ned? Will he still call me Papa?"

Billy hadn't thought about that. "I guess." He paused. "And Sal's little. She can still call you Papa."

"What about Mama? Will you call her Mom?"

Billy nodded slowly. "We can tell her together when she comes home from school."

They fell silent. Billy chose another cookie and bit into it. He looked at Papa, taking him in. It was strange—Billy wanted to call him Dad, but he still thought of him as Papa.

Papa broke the silence. "Let's practice," he said. "Hi, Billy."

Billy hesitated. "Hi—Dad." His voice was just a thread of itself. Saying the word *Dad* felt odd.

"Again," said Papa. "Hi, Billy."

"Hi, Dad."

They did it again and again and again, louder and faster, their voices overlapping, getting silly, until they were laughing. Then Papa said, "You're shredding my heart." But Billy was still laughing—and he didn't know how to respond anyway—and so he took a deep breath and just kept laughing.

There. He'd done it. With Papa's help. And it was no big deal.

When Mama had come home from work, Billy and Papa had told her that Billy wanted to call her Mom from now on.

"Really?" she'd said, a trace of sadness in her voice. "Really, truly?"

Billy and Papa nodded at the same time.

"I'm Dad," said Papa.

Mama put her bag of school things on the

floor, sat on a kitchen chair, and pulled Billy to her. She hugged him, and in the most natural way, said, "I guess you're growing up."

"Yup," he said, squirming away from the hug.

Done.

Sal, who was not yet fully emerged from her nap, had shuffled into the kitchen during the middle of the conversation, her eyes still sleepy. She seemed oblivious to what was really happening. She pointed to everybody, one by one. "You're Billy. You're Papa. You're Mama. I'm me." As if under a spell, Sal grabbed a cookie and climbed onto Mama's lap, melting into her. Sal's eyelids fluttered, fighting to stay open. Her grip on the cookie loosened.

"Come with me," Papa said quietly to Billy. "I want to show you something." He rescued Sal's cookie before it dropped to the floor. He snapped it in two and pressed one half in Billy's hand. "For the road," he said.

They didn't go far. Just to the garage.

The first thing Papa did was to turn off the radio. Billy noticed that the cello with arms had been pushed against the wall, partially draped with a blanket, abandoned.

"All right," said Papa, clapping his hands. "I wouldn't call it a breakthrough yet, but I've been working hard today. Because of you."

Laid out on the table in Papa's work area were several wooden cigar boxes. Each one had various items placed inside it. The inside of one box resembled a landscape, another a city. One looked like a funny face with mismatched watch dial eyes, a doorknob nose, and a black plastic comb mustache. The boxes were in differing stages of completion.

"I've just begun," explained Papa. "At this point, I'm just moving things around, trying things out. Nothing's close to being finished."

"They're dioramas!" said Billy. He grinned. "I helped you—I gave you the idea."

"You did," said Papa, smiling. "And I thank you. I'm calling them assemblages, but that's just a fancy way of saying they're dioramas."

Billy felt taller somehow. Bigger. Shiny, even. He'd never helped Papa in such an important way before.

Papa had all kinds of things on hand to use for his assemblages: bolts, nails, wire, marbles, foreign coins, twigs, fabric scraps,

beads, shards of glass, seashells, stones, old black-and-white photographs, maps. These things were on the table—in jars, little heaps, and stacks—surrounding the boxes.

"Check out this one," said Papa. He directed Billy's attention to the box at the corner of his worktable.

102

It was a face—a realistic-looking one—with green sea-glass eyes, coils of wire for hair, and an intricate arrangement of small pieces of wood for skin.

"I'm not done with it yet," said Papa.

Suddenly, the face came into clear focus. In wonder, Billy said, "It's me!"

"Yes, it is," said Papa. "If it turns out, I might do one of Mama and Sal, too."

"You're so good," said Billy. "When I'm older, I hope I'm good at something."

"You will be," said Papa. "And you're already good at many things."

Billy waited to hear what the things were, but Papa just smiled at him before making some adjustments on one of the boxes.

They shared a pleasant, companionable silence. Then Papa ruffled Billy's hair. Billy could feel Papa's fingers lingering, searching, like when he checked for ticks after they went hiking or camping.

"Hey, mister," Papa said, "you are lump free."

Strangely, it was as if Papa's words were coming through his fingers and from all around, pressing against Billy. And Billy felt the full force of Papa's attention.

Billy hadn't thought about his lump in a while. He raised his hand and felt for himself. It was true. His lump was gone. A fact. "Let's tell everyone," he said.

"Let's," said Papa. "And after that, you

can help me make dinner."

"Can we have macaroni and cheese?"

"I think that could be arranged," said Papa. With his arms stretched wide, he guided Billy out of the garage. "You're a good boy. A good lump-free boy."

"Thank you, Papa, yes I am."

"Hey, what about *Dad*? I thought I was Dad?"

"Oh—" said Billy. "I forgot." He paused. He puckered his lips, then bit his lower one, released it. "I might forget sometimes," he admitted.

"That's okay," said Papa. "You might forget what to call me, but I know you know who I am," he joked.

Billy grabbed Papa's sleeve. He stared up at him. "Don't worry, Dad," he said. "I'll never forget you."

"I'm not worried," said Papa. "Not one little bit."

And they went into the house, side by side, to spread their good news.

PART THREE

SISTER

1

Billy Miller hated his sister. At least, right now he did. Sal was crying—wailing, really—so loudly that Billy had gone to his room, shut the door, flung himself on his bed, and buried his head under his pillow. The crying continued and Billy could not escape it. The sound penetrated the pillow, then it seemed to be coming from deep inside him like an extra, throbbing, irritating pulse.

Finally, the crying stopped. Billy didn't

believe it at first. He pushed aside his pillow and cocked his head. Nothing. He rolled off his bed and tiptoed to the door. He opened it a crack. Not a sound.

Tentatively, he headed downstairs to check out the situation. He stopped on the landing and looked out the window. It was dark. The  streetlight at the corner was on, illuminating the falling snow. Like dandelion fluff, the snow drifted slowly to the ground, and Billy continued quietly down to the living room.

Sal was on the couch nestled against Gabby, Sal and Billy's babysitter. Sal was silent, but her body was heaving and shuddering in an oddly rhythmic pattern. Gabby was stroking Sal's hair. When Gabby saw Billy she gave him a thumbs-up sign.

"Ruby's Cupboard is back on schedule," said Gabby. "If you're still up for it."

"Yes," said Billy.

"Good," said Gabby. "I'm hungry. I'll help Sal wash up and then we can go."

Sal lifted her head and swiveled it like a periscope. She seemed to be searching, seeing if Mama and Papa had magically reappeared. Her eyes were red-rimmed and her cheeks were splotchy. "I cried so much I'm washed enough," she said in a hoarse whisper.

"Good point," said Gabby. She prodded Sal

playfully. "Well, let's get our coats and hats and mittens on."

Billy was ready in a flash. Maybe part of the evening could be salvaged. He'd had a vision as to how this night was going to be, and mostly his vision had crumbled to pieces.

It was Friday. Mama and Papa had driven to Chicago for a party at the gallery that was showing Papa's new artwork, his assemblages. They were going to stay at a hotel in Chicago and return the next afternoon.

The plan had been that Ned was going to spend the night at Billy's house. Gabby was going to take Billy, Ned, and Sal out for dinner. They'd have hot dogs, onion rings, and root beer. Dessert would be ice cream sundaes. And, most exciting, Billy and Ned were going to stay awake all night—something Billy had never done before. This part of the plan was a secret.

But Ned had thrown up at school during the afternoon recess, and even though he'd sworn on the phone from home that he felt fine, Mama canceled the sleepover. "I don't want you or Sal getting sick," she'd said to Billy, checking his forehead for a temperature. "Gabby will still take you to Ruby's Cupboard. You'll still have a good time."

Billy had tried to adjust his attitude. He

reminded himself how much he loved to eat out, and he reminded himself that he could stay up all night without Ned. Why not? It would still be one of the major events of his life.

But then as Mama and Papa drove away, Sal burst into tears. A delayed reaction. It was as if something inside her suddenly broke or popped or was switched on. She was hysterical. Gabby, Billy, and even the Drop Sisters were powerless to soothe her.

The gushing of tears went on.

And on.

And on.

Billy couldn't stand it. He put his hands over his ears. He'd gone from trying to be helpful, to being annoyed, to feeling angry. "CAN. WE. GO. NOW. PLEASE?" he repeated loudly over the relentless crying.

"I'm working on it," Gabby said calmly. "We just might have to eat here," she told Billy.

Billy curled his lip. "NO," he said. He stormed up to his room, hiding and seething. And that's where he'd stayed until the crying had stopped.

At last, things were back on track. Gabby was driving Billy, Sal, and the Drop Sisters to Ruby's Cupboard in her car.

"Isn't the snow pretty?" asked Gabby. "It's so feathery. Like snow in a movie."

"It's furry," said Billy, staring out the window.

When he'd stepped out of the house, it was as if a curtain of peacefulness had fallen over the neighborhood. It was quiet. The air smelled wet and white.

"Will Ruby's still be open?" asked Billy.

"Definitely," said Gabby. "It's not *that* late."

To Billy, it seemed that Sal had cried for hours. He was starving. "Are you going to get a hot dog?" he asked Sal.

Instead of saying yes or no, Sal responded with a sad whimper.

"Is everything okay, Salamander?" asked Gabby.

Sal sniffled. "I'm okay. It was just a left-over cry." She sniffled again. "But the Drop Sisters might cry. I just told them that Mama and Papa are gone."

Billy pinched his eyes closed with his thumb and index finger. Oh no, he thought. Here we go again.

But right after that, they pulled into the parking lot. Gabby said, "We're here!" And to Billy's great relief, Sal let out a little squeak of joy.

2

Once inside the restaurant, Sal was a different person. She became chatty and playful, almost giddy. "I love it here," she said. "I really, really *love* it here. So do the girls." She kissed the Drop Sisters one by one, then plunked each down on the seat beside her. Gabby had requested a booth to accommodate the Drop Sisters, which also made enough space for everyone's mittens, hats, scarves, and puffy winter jackets.

"There sure is a lot to look at," said Gabby. "It's like being inside a pinball machine."

Billy was mesmerized. They were surrounded by blinking lights, paper lanterns, and flickering traffic signs. A train ran

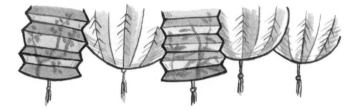

continuously on a track around the room. The track was attached to a ledge that was mounted to the wall. Brightly colored, miniature hot air balloons inched back and forth on wires overhead, crisscrossing the ceiling. And large papier-mâché animals were stationed between the tables. Billy's favorite was a lion whose mouth was open wide, show-ing a mountain range of jagged teeth.

But the best thing about Ruby's Cupboard was the food, especially the onion rings, which were as big as donuts. It was the kind of food Mama and Papa didn't approve of, except on special occasions. So, Billy tried to enjoy every single second of every single mouthful.

While they were eating their hot fudge sundaes, the family at the table next to theirs broke into a lively rendition of "Happy Birthday."

"*We* should celebrate something," said Sal.

"No singing," said Billy. He did *not* want to be embarrassed.

"We could celebrate your dad's show or the beautiful snowfall," Gabby suggested.

"We could celebrate *me*," said Sal.

"I know!" said Billy. "We can celebrate the Year of the Dragon. I'll show you." He searched for his jacket and dug into one of the pockets. He pulled out two things: an envelope and a pearl. "I almost forgot about these."

"What is it?" asked Sal. Her eyes had zeroed in on the pearl.

"Ms. Silver told us about the Year of the Dragon today. The Chinese New Year started on Monday. It's different than our New Year because theirs is lunar, which means the moon," Billy explained. "We didn't do anything special at school for the Year of the Rabbit, so Ms. Silver had a dragon party today. We ate tangerines because they're a symbol of good luck. And we watched Chinese dancers on the computer."

Billy paused, trying to remember everything Ms. Silver had taught them. "The dragon can have the head of a donkey and the body of a snake. Or it can just be a dragon."

"But what's *that*?" Sal asked, still focused on the pearl.

"Oh," said Billy. "The dragon carries a pearl in its claws. The pearl means it has supernatural powers. So, Ms. Silver gave one to everybody." He held up the pearl and rolled it between his fingers. "It's magic." He acted as if the pearl were coming to life in his hand.

"What's the envelope?" asked Gabby.

"It's an empty envelope, but it has a dragon stamp on it. It's official—a real stamp. Ms. Silver's brother works at the post office. See?" Billy presented the envelope so that Gabby and Sal could look at the dragon stamp.  "Ms. Silver said we should write a letter to someone."

"To wish them a happy lunar New Year?" asked Gabby.

"Sure," said Billy. "Or, Ms. Silver said we could use it for a thank you note or to tell someone you appreciate them. She said no one writes letters anymore, and it's a nice thing to do."

"You could write Ms. Silver a thank you note for the envelope," said Sal.

Gabby smiled.

Billy shot Sal a dismissive look.

"Can I have the pearl?" asked Sal.

"Nope," said Billy.

Gabby clapped her hands. "Okay, everyone get a big spoonful of ice cream. On the count of three we'll eat them. Then make a dragon face and roar—softly. And we'll have a good year."

Gabby counted. They all ate. They all made dragon faces. They roared.

"I couldn't eat another bite," said Gabby. She pushed away the remains of her sundae. She sighed loudly and placed her hands on her belly.

"Do you have a food baby?" asked Billy.

Gabby laughed. "I think I do," she said. "Where did you learn that expression?"

"Kids say it at school."

"What's a food baby?" asked Sal.

"It's when you eat so much," said Billy, "your stomach feels big and you feel like you're having a baby."

"Boys can't have babies," said Sal.

"Boys can have food babies," said Billy.

"Okay, you two, let's bundle up and go home," said Gabby.

It took them a while to dress for outside.

"Can I get a cup of coffee to go?" Billy asked Gabby as he adjusted his scarf.

"Are you crazy?" she said. "You don't drink coffee. And you'd be up all night."

That's my plan, thought Billy.

Gabby tugged Billy's knitted cap over his eyes, then pulled it up and flashed him a toothy grin. "You're funny," she said. She tossed the pillowcase with the Drop Sisters over her shoulder, like Santa Claus with his bag of toys, and led the way out the door and into the wintry world.

"It's cold!" said Sal.

It was. And Billy felt the cold press against his face, stinging his eyes and nose, but deep within himself he felt a core of warmth— because of the food and because he was getting excited about staying up all night.

As they tramped to the car, Sal tweaked Billy's jacket sleeve. Snowflakes were catching in her eyelashes, turning them to lace. "What are you going to do with the magic pearl?" she asked.

"I don't know," said Billy. And he truly didn't. But he did know one thing—he was not going to give it to Sal. He didn't really think the pearl had supernatural powers, but *she* thought so. And that made the pearl very powerful indeed.

Billy crept along the hallway and turned the corner. The strip of golden light that had been shining from beneath the guest-room door was gone, meaning Gabby was asleep. Billy crept back to his room and quietly shut the door. He switched on his bedside lamp, then jammed a sweatshirt under the door so the light wouldn't leak into the hallway, drawing attention to himself, exposing his plan.

Sal had been asleep for a long time. Like

a tree dropping its leaves all at once, she'd collapsed in a heap on the sofa right after they'd returned from the restaurant. She was probably exhausted from all her crying. Or from asking Billy if she could have his magic pearl, which she'd done about a dozen times in the car on the ride home.

After Gabby had carried Sal up to bed, Billy showed Gabby his Christmas presents. Then they played Crazy Eights. Gabby yawned frequently, covering her mouth with the fan of cards she held.

Billy wished that Gabby would stop yawning. It was contagious. He began yawning, too, and felt himself growing sleepy—the last thing he wanted to be.

"One more hand," said Gabby. "Then bed." She yawned again.

"Already?" asked Billy. "I thought we could watch a movie or play a board game." His eyes were pleading.

"Oh, Billy, I can't," said Gabby. "It's late. And you're yawning, too."

"We could have a snack," Billy suggested.

"Are you kidding?" said Gabby. "I'm so full from dinner I feel like I'll never eat again. I still have my food baby," she said with a chuckle, tipping her head and casting her eyes downward. "Seriously, are you hungry already?"

"Not really. But if you were, I'd sit with you while you ate."

Gabby twisted her wrist to check her watch. Her bracelets—inches of them, silver and gold, surrounding the watch—jingled. She looked him up and down. "I'm sorry, Billy Boy, but it's time for bed."

"Wait—you said one more hand."

"Okay," said Gabby. "A quick one."

During their final hand, Billy held back from playing certain cards when he could  have won, prolonging the game as long as possible. But soon Gabby was the winner and he was off to bed.

He went to the bathroom and brushed his teeth. He put on his pajamas and crawled under his covers. He said good night to Gabby and waited.

And waited.

And waited.

When the house was quiet, he checked to see if the light in the guest room was still on. It was. So he went back to his room and waited some more. When he checked again, the light was out.

And, now, here he was, in his room, ready to begin the night of staying awake.

He told himself he could do this. He felt a shiver of excitement, then a buzzy sensation. If he made it through the night without sleeping, he'd be a different person, somehow. A more important person.

His eyelids were the problem—they were as heavy as steel. The situation was worse if he lay down, so he rose from his bed and paced around his room. But the bed was so inviting—soft, warm—that he couldn't help taking a break, allowing himself only to sit on it.

He turned his bedside lamp off and on and off and on. He tried to read. He tried to draw. He tried counting backward from one thousand.

He looked at the dragon stamp on the envelope from Ms. Silver. Then he took the pearl in his open palm and stared at it until it blurred. He pretended it really was magic.

"Stay awake," he whispered. "Stay awake."

Just then an idea came to him. Billy's idea was to scare himself so badly he couldn't sleep. He turned off the lights and sat in the dark on his bed, resting his back against the wall, his legs crisscrossed into a pretzel. He tried to imagine the worst possible things he could.

He envisioned a life on his own without Mama and Papa, but that just made him sad. *Think*. A few memorably frightening scenes from movies danced before his eyes. *Think*. Some of the pictures in Papa's big, thick art books were weird and made him uneasy; he recalled them as best he could.

Think.

He began to convince himself that there was something hiding in the black space beneath his bed.

Think.

The something had white melted flesh with oozing clusters of pimples for eyes. Its nose was a wet hole that made a whistling noise with each breath. It had long, stringy gray hair and thin, knobby fingers and bloody sores all over its naked body. It creaked and rattled and groaned. The thing ate children. Its teeth were sharp as needles. It was stretching and reaching, reaching and stretching. Creeping. Right under him.

The mattress groaned.

The wind whistled.

The radiator rattled.

The house creaked.

The curtains moved.

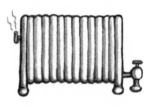

The shadows vibrated.

Billy found it hard to breathe. His heart was pounding. He still had the pearl in his hand and his grip around it was so tight his knuckles hurt.

Awful things were where they didn't belong. Awful things were hidden everywhere.

Billy repositioned himself; his bedspread pulled as if something were grabbing it from below. Then his room tilted and the walls started closing in on him.

Billy sprang from his bed and bolted out of his room. He stopped suddenly. What should he do? Where should he go? He didn't want Gabby to think he was a baby. He fled down the hall and threw open the door. "Sal," he said, his voice soft, but frantic and breaking. "Sal, wake up."

4

Sal's night-light was so bright that the yellow walls in her room glowed like the inside of  a jack-o'-lantern and had an instant calming effect on Billy. The only visible part of Sal among her pillows, the Drop Sisters, and her messy blankets was her snarl of dark curls, but it was a familiar snarl and Billy's heart slowed down; his breathing steadied.

Billy sat on the bed and bounced. The dark snarl moved a little. Billy knew his question was the dumbest in the world, but he asked it anyway. "Are you sleeping?"

The snarl moved again.

Billy bounced harder, and then Sal's head emerged from the shadowy lumps and bumps of bedclothes and stuffed animals like a chick from an egg. She looked at him with uncertain eyes—slits, really.

Billy scooched nearer to Sal. He didn't know what to say. He couldn't say *I need you*, which was the truth. "Hi," he whispered.

Sal's eyes closed and her head drooped. Billy shook her. It was strange, but already he felt less afraid. How could a three-year-old make him feel safe? Especially one who was mostly asleep. Although part of him knew there was no monster under his bed, he did not want to go back to his room. He wanted to stay here.

Billy shook Sal again and blew at her eyes. When she opened them, he blew again. He'd been holding the pearl the whole time, and now he raised it up to Sal's face, inches away from her nose. "Sal, look," he said. "It's the magic pearl. And, I'll give it to you *if*—"

Sal perked up. Her eyes widened. "You will?" She reached greedily for the pearl.

"*If*—" said Billy, pulling the pearl back a bit.

"If what?"

Billy's brain had clicked back to his plan to

142

stay up all night. He could not do it alone in his room. But he thought he could do it in Sal's room. With her. He'd never shared anything this big with a girl before, but it would be worth it.

"If you can stay up all night with me, it's yours," said Billy.

"Why?" asked Sal.

Billy explained the importance of his idea. He finished by reminding her, "We've never even made it to midnight on New Year's Eve." He kept holding up the pearl as if it were a priceless gem, turning it between his fingers, hypnotizing her with it.

"Can I have it now?" she asked.

"You can borrow it," said Billy. "But you can't have it until morning."

"How long is it till tomorrow?" asked Sal.

It was a good question. "I'll find out," said Billy. He went to check the digital clock in the bathroom. He was relieved that he didn't have to pass his room to get there; still, he was cautious and quick. The red numbers on the clock were clear and bright: 10:32. We've got a long way to go, he thought, feeling some of his optimism drain away.

Back in Sal's room, he crammed her throw rug under the door and flipped on her overhead light. They both blinked, adjusting to the change. "Now it'll be easier to stay awake," he told her.

Sal was fingering the pearl with loving

care. "How long till tomorrow?" she asked again.

"A long time," said Billy. "But we can do it. It's only an hour and a half until midnight."

"What are we going to do?" asked Sal.

"What do you want to do?"

"We could play with the Drop Sisters," said Sal.

"Will that keep you awake more than anything else?" asked Billy. He was willing to do whatever it took to achieve his goal.

Sal nodded.

"Okay," said Billy. "How do we play with them?"

"You tell a story about them. And you move them around. Like this." Sal slid off her bed, pulling the Drop Sisters with her. She placed them in a circle on the floor. She picked up Raindrop and swooped her back and forth through the air. "One day Raindrop flew. 'I'm a bird! I'm a bird!'"

"Shh," Billy murmured.

"Your turn," said Sal.

Billy chose one of the Drop Sisters. He didn't think he could do this. He felt self-conscious. He wouldn't want Ned to see him now. Or Emma. He sighed. Finally, he said, "One day there was a big explosion, and the unlucky Drop Sister felt the jolt, like lightning." He tossed the stuffed whale up a few feet and let it fall and tumble. "She was stunned," he said. "Then the doctors came to do CPR." Billy took his fist and pumped the unlucky Drop Sister's midsection, quietly grunting with each thrust.

"Stop," said Sal. "You're hurting her. It's okay, Gumdrop." She pulled Gumdrop to safety on her lap. "You didn't even know her name," she scolded, glaring at Billy.

"Sorry," said Billy.

"Papa knows all their names." Sal gathered the other Drop Sisters and piled them on and around her. "Maybe you could just tell a story and not touch them." Her arms circled them, protecting them. "No more explosions."

Billy wasn't good at telling stories, the way Papa was. He was better at *doing* things. He had a feeling that this night would be longer than he had imagined. He glanced around the room with the hope that something on Sal's walls or shelves would trigger an idea.

Billy noticed that Sal's eyelids were lowering again. "Hey, Sal, can I use that?" He motioned to the dingy pillowcase in which she carried the Drop Sisters. It was crumpled up at the foot of the bed.

"What are you going to do with it?"

"It's a surprise. You'll like it. Can I use it?"

Sal considered Billy's question.

"Remember—the pearl," Billy said, even though he knew one had absolutely nothing to do with the other.

"All right," said Sal.

Billy took the pillowcase, filled it with

148

clothes from Sal's dresser, and bound the open end with one of her stretchy hair bands, twisting it around and around. He'd left several inches of cloth at the end; he fanned it out. "This is the tail," he said.

Then he pushed and pulled and fluffed the stuffed pillowcase until it pleased him. "There," he said. "It's a whale. A big one."

"It *is*," said Sal. "Who is it?"

"This is—" Billy said, thinking fast. "This is—*Cough*drop. He's the Drop Sisters' cousin. He usually lives at the aquarium. But he's here for a visit."

"Coughdrop," said Sal, smiling. "I love him. Make him say something."

"He doesn't talk," said Billy, "because he

has a terrible cough. He was born with it. And the only food he eats is cough drops."

Sal plucked Coughdrop from Billy's hands and introduced him to his cousins.

They played. Sal would make a comment as one of the Drop Sisters, then Billy, assuming the role of Coughdrop, would cough in response. They took turns "talking," having a conversation until Billy had had enough. "Coughdrop needs a break," he said.

Billy was exhausted and his throat was rough. He decided that he would never be a babysitter, no matter how much money he could make.

"Is it morning yet?" asked Sal.

"No," said Billy. "I'll go check again."

And then Sal said something, but she was yawning at the same time and she'd put her hand over her mouth, so all Billy heard was a tired little noise.

When he came back to Sal's room with the disappointing news that it was only 11:03, Sal was sleeping on the floor beside the Drop Sisters, her head on Coughdrop.

Billy made very little effort to wake her. He made very little effort to do anything. He couldn't. All at once it felt as if his pajamas were made of lead. His legs could barely hold him up and it took everything he had in him to drag some blankets off Sal's bed, fall to the floor next to her, and cover both of them.

He would give it one more try. He raised

151

his head and opened his eyes as wide as he could. "Stay awake," he commanded himself. A swift, invisible hand pressed his head down and stitched his eyes shut. He tried to conjure up an image of the monster under his bed, but he didn't even have the energy for that. His head knocked into Sal's as he searched for some comfort on Coughdrop.

Sal stirred. "Love you," she murmured.

She could have been talking to the Drop Sisters or Coughdrop or him. He didn't know. But he knew he loved her. Right now, anyway. And he might have told her so, but all he could manage was to mutter "Yeah" as he drifted off to sleep.

152

5

"Wake up, sleepyheads," said Gabby.

Billy blinked. For a moment he had no clue where he was. He stretched. Like a bubble rising through murky water to sunlight above, he slowly worked his way to being fully awake and aware.

He remembered the night and his failed attempt to stay up until morning—and it disappointed him. He felt he had been cheated out of something that should have been his.

"Is it tomorrow?" peeped Sal.

"It's almost lunchtime," said Gabby. "Your mom called from the road. They'll be home in about an hour." Gabby kissed the tops of both of their heads. "Your dad called earlier to see how the night went. He said to let you sleep in. But I never thought you'd sleep *this* late. When your mom called, she said to wake you up."

"How was Dad's show?" asked Billy.

"*Papa's* show," said Sal.

"He said he sold five pieces," Gabby told them. "He sounded happy." She scooped up the nest of blankets from the floor. "Let's get your rooms in shape before they get here." She turned toward Billy. "When did you come to Sal's room?" she asked. "I checked on Sal when I got up and was surprised to see you."

"I'm not sure."

"Were you afraid?"

"Nope."

"You know you can always wake me up."

Billy did a combination nod and shrug.

Gabby started making Sal's bed. She shook out one of the blankets. The pearl had been caught up in its folds. As the blanket ballooned and settled on the mattress, the pearl shot across the room, hit the wall, and magically rolled to a stop at Sal's feet.

"The pearl!" cried Sal, raising herself up and down on her toes. "I forgot it." She picked it up and brought it to Billy. "Did we make it to morning?"

He flicked her a look that said *You're crazy.* He extended his open hand and motioned for her to give up the pearl.

"Did we make it to *midnight*?" she asked, slipping her hand with the pearl behind her back. Her voice sounded as if she knew the answer.

"What are you two talking about?" asked Gabby as she smoothed out the bedspread.

"Nothing," replied Billy.

"And what is this?" Gabby was holding up Coughdrop by his tail. "Were you planning on running away in the middle of the night? Is this your pack of provisions?"

156

"That's Coughdrop!" said Sal. "Billy made him for me. He's the Drop Sisters' cousin. He just eats cough drops and he can't talk."

Gabby laughed. "You are clever, Billy Boy. And smart. I didn't know anything about the Year of the Dragon until last night."

"Soon will *I* learn everything?" asked Sal.

"Yes, you will," said Gabby.

Gabby told them to get dressed and hurry down to the kitchen. "I can make you something to eat right away, or we can make a big brunch and wait for your parents to get here."

"Brunch," said Billy.

"Brunch," said Sal.

"Meet me in the kitchen," said Gabby.

Billy and Sal were alone. Their eyes connected and they exchanged a meaningful look. Then Sal reached out reluctantly to Billy. She gave him the pearl and she gave him the most forlorn expression imaginable.

"I tried to stay awake," she said.

"Me, too," said Billy. "I almost did it."

"Did *you* make it to midnight?"

"I might have. I'm not sure. I *think* so."

They stood together in silence.

Billy's forehead wrinkled in thought. These were the things he was thinking: I don't really care about the pearl. Sal helped me last night—but I can't tell her that. If I give her the pearl, it would be a way to thank her without having to say anything.

"Here," he said. "You can have the pearl, Sal."

Sal took the pearl and kissed it. "Thank you, Billy!" She hopped with glee and did a little dance, pulling up her nightgown by its hem and swishing it about.

"See you downstairs," he called as he left.

He dressed quickly and straightened his room. He looked under his bed, just because. Nothing was there, of course.

His mind was ricocheting from one thing to the next. He wondered if Mama would let him play with Ned today. He wondered what Gabby was making for brunch. He hoped that Mama and Papa didn't go away over-night again for a long time. When they were both gone, the air in the house was harder to breathe, somehow.

He moved the envelope with the dragon stamp to the middle of his desk. He wanted to get down to the kitchen fast; he could hear the promising sound of pots and pans. But he decided to do something first. He tore a piece of paper from the notebook in his backpack and wrote a letter to put in the envelope and mail.

The letter said:

Dear Sal,

Will make it to morning next time. Your ok.

Your brother,

Billy

He knew that she couldn't read the letter by herself, but he thought she'd like it anyway. As he was stuffing it into the envelope, he heard joyful shrieks coming from below. Sal. He didn't want to be left out of anything. The envelope could be addressed and sealed and sent later. And now? Now he could sail downstairs to see what the day would bring.

PART FOUR

MOTHER

1

The month of May had been so hot and dry, Billy wondered if the whole town would shrivel up. The blistering day he came home from school with his problem, Sal was sitting in the shade on the front porch holding a bag of frozen blueberries against her skin to keep cool. Billy could tell that she'd also been eating the blueberries because her fingers and face were stained purple.

"Papa's inside," said Sal. "By the conditioning."

"*Air*-conditioning," Billy corrected.

There was no air-conditioning at school, and being in Room 2 was like spending time in an oven. Billy's clothes had been sticking to his chair all afternoon, making it hard to concentrate on anything but his own 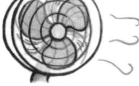 discomfort. Ms. Silver kept the windows and door open and she had a big fan running continuously, but it didn't help much.

"The Drop Sisters are inside, too," said Sal. She pressed the sweaty bag to her cheek and then her leg. "Papa put the girls away until I'm done with the blueberries. So I don't get them dirty."

Billy stepped past Sal and opened the front door. The cool air was a great relief. "Hi, Dad," he called as he dropped onto the couch and lay down. "Ahh," he murmured. He felt so comfortable he forgot about his problem until Papa entered the room and asked, "How was your day?"

Billy sat up. "I have a little problem."

"I'm glad it's little," said Papa. "What is it?"

Billy didn't know where to start. He realized that often the beginning of a problem goes back, and back further, to something that doesn't seem like a problem at all. He could feel Papa watching him, waiting.

"Well?" said Papa.

"Well, this year Ms. Silver wants to do a show for the end of the year. But not a play like *The Three Billy Goats Gruff* or *The Emperor's New Clothes*, because she's done that before."

Papa nodded.

"She wants to do something original. With poetry." Billy didn't particularly like poetry, except funny poetry, but that wasn't the problem. "Everyone has to write a poem about someone in their family. Ms. Silver said the show would be called *Family* or *Room 2 Families* or something like that."

"Sounds nice."

"The poem can be about a parent or a brother or a sister or a grandma or an uncle or someone who helps your family like a good friend, because all families are different." Billy took a breath. "Then when we have the show, we have to say our poem on the stage with a microphone and you can memorize it if you want to."

"Is that the problem?" asked Papa. "Memorizing?"

"No," said Billy. "The problem is that we're supposed to write about *one* person, and that *one* person can be with us on the stage. But only one. So I have to choose. . . . "

"Ah," said Papa. "I get it."

"I have to pick you or Mom or Sal."

Papa pursed his lips. He glanced out the window at Sal, then he turned his head

169

back toward Billy. "I don't think having Sal up on a stage with a microphone would be a good idea," said Papa. "She might do something—unexpected." Papa blinked. "I think you should limit your choice to Mama or me."

"Is that okay?" asked Billy. It seemed that excluding Sal was like lying somehow. And it felt strange to have Papa suggest it.

"Yes," said Papa. "I think it's okay."

Billy's problem was smaller now, but he still had a problem. He still had to choose between Mama and Papa. He didn't want either one to feel bad.

Papa seemed to have a window into Billy's thoughts. "If you pick Mama, that's fine with me. And if you pick me, it will be fine with Mama. Remember that."

"Member what?" asked Sal, who'd just popped up behind Papa like a Whac-A-Mole at the county fair.

Papa turned. "Remember not to touch anything until you wash your blueberry hands. And don't you dare kiss me with those blueberry lips." He snatched up Sal and hauled her off to the kitchen, her giggles trailing behind them.

Billy sat alone, considering the choice he had to make. He sucked the web of skin between his thumb and pointer finger, his hand falling across his chin like a beard.

ᄋᆞᄋ

Mama was so hot when she came home from work that all she wanted to do was take a cool shower. Then she made lemonade with Sal. By the time Mama called him for dinner, Billy hadn't found the right moment to tell her much about the show, except that there was going to be one.

But, he had made his decision. He'd decided that he would choose her. Mama. She would be the one he would write a poem about. She would be the one he would share the stage with.

It would be easier to write a poem about a boy (Papa), but Billy thought the whole thing would make Mama happier. She even taught poetry. Also, Papa volunteered at Billy's

172

school sometimes and went on field trips, and Mama never could because she was teaching. This would be a way to make up for that.

Billy still felt uncomfortable about choosing one over the other, so he'd come up with a plan so that Papa wouldn't know he'd made a deliberate choice. His plan was to have Mama and Papa each pick a number from one to ten. Instead of having a particular number in mind and writing it down, he'd wait  for Mama and Papa to say their numbers, and then, no matter what number Mama chose, he would declare it the winner.

It wouldn't be fair, but that way Papa wouldn't have his feelings hurt. It was sort of the same thing as excluding Sal from the show without her knowing it. And Papa had said that that was okay.

During dinner, Mama asked question after question about the show. Billy explained everything, including how either she or Papa would be onstage with him.

"It sounds wonderful," Mama said. "Although I'd love a play with cute animals. You'd be adorable with whiskers, little furry ears, and a pink nose."

Billy scrunched up his face. "No way."

"Can I go?" asked Sal.

"Of course," said Papa.

"There'll be refreshments, too," Billy told them.

Then Billy said to Mama and Papa, "Now, Mom, Dad, pick a number. From one to ten. The person who's closest wins. I'll write a poem about you."

"Five," said Mama, without hesitating.

"Six," said Papa.

"Five was the *exact* number," said Billy, trying to be as natural as possible, trying to convince himself that five would have been the number he would have selected. His ears were burning, and he worried that they were turning red. His cheeks, too. He formed a fish mouth and looked around the room because he couldn't make direct eye contact with anyone.

"Hooray for me," said Mama. She blew Billy a kiss across the table.

Papa smiled as if *he'd* won.

"Hooray for Mama!" said Sal. She threw out her arms cheerfully and accidentally knocked her plate to the floor.

Nothing broke, but applesauce, buttered noodles, and steamed carrots were everywhere. And, so, much to Billy's relief, everyone's attention shifted to the mess and to cleaning up.

Billy sighed. He realized that as soon as one problem is solved, something else is right there, waiting to take up your time. He'd solved the problem of who to choose. But, now, of course, he had a poem to write.

176

2

Because of the upcoming show, Ms. Silver was spending a lot of time on poetry. She read several poems a day—all different kinds. No matter how hot it was, she turned off the big fan when she read so that everyone could hear her.

Billy knew he liked funny poems. Poems about underwear or pranks or food fights. He discovered that he also liked poems about aliens and volcanoes. He liked some of the animal poems Ms. Silver read, especially one that was about a bat. Billy thought that a funny bat poem that included a food fight and a volcano would be the best poem ever.

Ms. Silver gave everyone in Room 2 a new notebook. "These are your poetry journals,"  she told them. "We'll use them to write our poems for our show. Then you can keep them to use over the summer. For writing or drawing or whatever you want. But, I hope you'll continue to think about poetry even when school is done for the year."

Writing a poem about Mama would not be easy to do. Ms. Silver said that the poems *could* be funny, but that they had to be appropriate.

She said to think of the poems as a nice way to honor a special person. Billy wanted to make sure that whatever he wrote pleased Mama. But he also wanted to make sure that whatever he wrote wouldn't embarrass him when he read it in front of a roomful of people including adults and his classmates.

Billy liked the rhythm and rhyming of limericks, but he thought it would be easier to write a haiku about Mama, or an acrostic. Or, he could write what Ms. Silver called free verse, which seemed to Billy to be ordinary writing just broken up into lines that were shorter than normal.

Billy did want to keep the poem short in case he tried to memorize it. Short was

179

also good because that would mean fewer words he might not be able to spell.

Ms. Silver's plan was that the students would work on their poems for a little while each day during writing time. Ms. Silver would walk around the room, checking the poems and helping with spelling. If she thought a poem was ready for the show, she'd draw a smiley face on the top corner of the page. She hoped that by the middle of the next week, everyone would have a poem all set to go.

"Remember that all good writers are *re*writers," Ms. Silver said. "Fine writing takes good, hard work."

Billy had trouble getting started. He

opened his poetry journal to the first page and wrote: *My Mom*. He couldn't think of anything else to write, so he drew a series of volcanoes in progressive stages of exploding.

There was still enough space in the margin on the left-hand side of the paper to write the word *MOM* vertically, so Billy decided that he would try an acrostic. In a burst of inspiration he wrote:

My

Only

Mother

Poetry's not too bad, he thought. He could definitely memorize this poem. He returned to drawing volcanoes.

Suddenly, Billy felt a shadow fall upon him, as if a cloud had appeared out of nowhere blocking the sun. He looked up. It was Ms. Silver. Today her chopsticks were yellow.

"I'm done," said Billy.

"Already?" said Ms. Silver. "You're a fast worker."

Billy nodded.

"Who are you writing about?"

Billy moved his hand so she could read what he'd written.

Ms. Silver smiled broadly. "Good choice."

"Can I write about my dog?" Ned interrupted.

"Remember, no pets," replied Ms. Silver.

"Even if it has a human name?" asked Ned. "His name's Bob."

Ms. Silver tightened her lips and shook her head at Ned. Then she crouched down beside Billy so that they were at the same level.

"Do I get a smiley face?" asked Billy. He could tell by her expression that he probably wouldn't.

"Maybe you could tell me more about your mom. What does she like? What makes her special?"

"Well," said Billy. "She *is* my only mom, so

I thought *that* made her special." He fumbled with his pencil. "Grace has *two* moms, and some moms, somewhere, must be dead, so that person wouldn't have *any* mom."

"That's true," said Ms. Silver. "Hmm." She coiled a loose strand of hair around one of her chopsticks. "Would you try writing a haiku for me? See what you can come up with." She moved on to help Ned.

Billy glanced at the posters on the bulletin board that showed the rules for writing different kinds of poems. He remembered that a haiku had three lines. The first and third lines each had five syllables and the middle line had seven. He turned to a new page in his notebook. He was still thinking about volcanoes, so he wrote:

Mom likes volcanos

They are hot and they explode

Please do not fall in

He was counting on his fingers, making sure he'd used the correct number of syllables, when Ms. Silver came back.

"May I take a peek?" she asked.

Billy chewed on his thumbnail while Ms. Silver read his poem.

"Does your mom like volcanoes?" asked Ms. Silver. "I know *you* like volcanoes."

"Well . . ." said Billy. "She *might*." He blinked rapidly.

"I have an idea," said Ms. Silver. "I think you should take your journal home tonight. You should ask your mom what she likes. You could make a list of things. The list could be your poem. Or, maybe, there's something you and your mom do together. You could write about that."

"Okay," said Billy. His eyes shifted down to his volcano drawings. He wasn't fond of homework in general, but it seemed even worse now that it was so close to the end of the school year. His mind was already focusing on summer vacation.

"You've done some fine writing today," said Ms. Silver. "We can work again tomorrow."

It really *is* work, thought Billy sadly.

When the dismissal bell rang, Billy noticed that most of his classmates, including Ned, were taking their journals home, too. He was glad he wasn't the only one.

Billy was in bed when he realized that he'd forgotten to work on his poem. His brain had been so full of other things, there hadn't been room for poetry.

When he came home from school, he and Ned had had a water fight. Then they tried to build a volcano in the garden. That led to making mud balls the size of oranges (to let dry and harden for future use). After that, Sal let them cover nearly every inch of her with mud. By that time Mama had come home. She and Papa decided that it was too hot to cook, so once Ned left and Sal and Billy were cleaned up, they went to Ruby's Cupboard for dinner as a very special, almost-the-end-of-the-school-year treat.

Being at Ruby's Cupboard reminded Billy of the time he'd tried to stay up all night. So, for the rest of the evening he was preoccupied with the idea of attempting it again, with Ned, as soon as summer vacation started. Poetry had been far from his mind, as remote as some unknown distant planet.

But now he couldn't force the thought of it away. He slipped out of bed, grabbed his poetry journal and a pencil, and went downstairs to look for Mama.

Mama was in the living room lying on the couch with her eyes shut. A paperback book, cracked open, was resting on her stomach like a little tent.

Billy didn't have to say a word—as he approached Mama her eyelids fluttered up. She closed her book, sat tall, patted the space beside her, and said, "Sit by me."

Billy did. "Where's Dad?" he asked.

"He's in the garage. He wanted to work a little longer before bed." She tipped her head toward his. "What's up? Trouble sleeping?"

MOTHER

Billy held up his poetry journal. "I was supposed to work on my poem about you." He paused. "I forgot."

"Do you have anything to show me?" asked Mama.

"I already wrote two poems, but Ms. Silver said to write another one."

"Let's see what you've got so far," said Mama.

After she read Billy's acrostic and haiku, Mama laughed softly. "I like them. You've got a great sense of humor, Billy Miller."

It was funny—if a parent used a kid's full name in movies or on TV, the parent was usually angry and the kid was in big trouble. But Mama and Papa often used his full name if they were complimenting him or being all lovey-dovey.

Billy turned to a clean page in his notebook. "Ms. Silver said I could write a list of things you like and that could be a poem. Poems don't have to rhyme, you know." He got his pencil ready. "Okay," he said. "What do you like?"

"Besides volcanoes?" Mama joked.

Billy smiled self-consciously.

"Okay," said Mama. "I like being with you. I love it, actually."

"*Mom.*"

"I know, you can't write *that* down. Well," she said, starting over, "I like coffee." She paused. "I like chocolate." She paused again. She was talking very slowly so that Billy could keep up with what she was saying. His pencil was moving fast. He could fix his spelling later. "I like rainy days." Pause. "I like—"

All of a sudden there was a thud. Something hit the window. They both jumped at the unexpected sound.

"What was that?" asked Billy. His heart was racing.

"I don't know," Mama replied in an uncertain voice.

Mama hurried to the window and Billy followed. It was difficult to see anything but their own reflections with the inside lights on, so Mama crossed the room to the front door. Billy was right behind her like her shadow. Mama held out her arm, making Billy wait as she turned on the porch light, opened the door, and looked around. Then she dropped her arm and walked slowly along the porch to the window.

"It's a bird," said Mama. "It must have been drawn by the light."

Billy joined her. There was a dark clump beneath the window on the porch floor. It was motionless.

"It's a robin," said Mama.

"Is it alive?" Billy whispered. He bit his lower lip and leaned closer.

194

"I don't think so," said Mama, crouching. "No."

Mama got her garden gloves and a shovel from the shed by the garage. She carried the dead bird and Billy carried the shovel to the corner of the garden.

"Should we get Papa?" asked Billy.

"No," said Mama. "We're fine."

It seemed to Billy that something big was happening.

Mama put the bird down. She dug a hole under a bush. Before she placed the bird in the hole, she held it at a certain angle in the light from the street lamp so that Billy could see it clearly one last time. The orange feathers seemed unreal, too beautiful to be part of something no longer alive.

The dead bird filled the hole as if it were filling a nest. Mama covered the bird with dirt and patted the dirt down. Billy found three stones and formed a triangle on top of the little mound.

They stood together. Neither talked. Billy hadn't noticed until now how hot it still was. His pajamas were damp with sweat. Dirt was sticking to his bare feet.

Mama broke the silence. "I like quiet," she said. "When it's quiet you can hear so much."

Billy looked up at her. "But then it's not quiet," he said.

"Listen," said Mama softly. She held her finger to her lips.

Billy listened. He didn't hear anything at first. Then he did. He heard insects and the sound of a sprinkler. He heard the leaves rustling overhead. He heard a car driving several streets over and a dog barking somewhere in the darkness.

It's quiet but it's not, thought Billy. Then he thought of the dead bird, and all the noises mixed together and grew louder in his head.

Mama squeezed his shoulders. "Of all the things I like, quiet might be my favorite."

A light moved slowly across the sky, far, far away. A lot of what Mama had said sounded like a poem. Billy hoped he could remember enough of it to write something down.

The world ticked and hummed and rushed around them. And they stood together a bit longer in the darkness.

This is the poem Billy wrote:

Quiet Mom
by Billy Miller

My mom likes a lot
She likes quiet best
Quiet can be loud if you lisen
It sounds like this
cars
sprinkelers
bugs

wind

dogs

Quiet is a dead bird

The next day Ms. Silver gave Billy's poem
a smiley face.

4

Billy was supposed to practice reading his poem aloud at home, but he didn't like practicing in front of Mama, Papa, or Sal. Mama thought he should practice in front of *someone*, so Papa pulled out his cello with the mannequin arms from his studio and moved it to Billy's room. "You can practice in front of this," said Papa. "I knew it would come in handy someday."

"It's better than nothing," said Mama,

laughing. "I think it's helpful to have an audience of some sort."

Billy took his baseball cap from their road trip the previous summer and put it on top of the cello. Papa made a sign that said I LOVE POETRY! and stuck it in one of the mannequin hands. Mama named the cello Poetry Man— and that's what every-one called it. Reading to Poetry Man was easier than reading  to a real person. Billy practiced every day.

Billy practiced every day at school, too. The second graders took turns reading their poems at the front of the room. There were three comments Ms. Silver repeated:

"Read slowly. Read loudly. Read with expression."

The students didn't have to memorize their poems, but they could if they wanted to. So far, just a few had chosen to do so. Emma was one of them. Billy was not.

"I have extra copies of each of your poems," said Ms. Silver. "I'll have a nice, new copy for you the night of the show, so don't worry if you leave your copy at home." She thought for a moment. "Oh, and even if you memorize your poem, I'd like you to take a copy with you up to the stage. That way, if you forget your words, you'll have them with you. This is a no-worries show."

Emma raised her hand. When she was

called on, she said, "I've memorized my poem so well I won't need a copy. I'm not boasting," she added. "It's just the truth."

"I'd like everyone to have a copy," said Ms. Silver evenly. "Just in case."

"When do we get to use the microphone?" asked Ned.

"Everyone will have a chance to try the microphone," said Ms. Silver. "We'll have at least one rehearsal with it before the day of the show."

Billy couldn't wait to try the microphone. When teachers used the microphone for announcements during lunch period, their voices were so big and booming they filled the cafeteria. Billy had never used a microphone.

He wondered what it would feel like to have a voice that big.

Room 2 was working hard on the show in other ways. The students painted a backdrop for the stage on large pieces of cardboard. They wrote the words WE ARE FAMILY—because that was the name of the show—in huge block letters, and patterned the background with squiggles, dots, and stars in all different colors.

Ms. Silver had to use her gong more than usual. "I think you've all got summeritis," she said.

"We've got showitis," Ned yelled.

Then Ms. Silver said, "I think Room Two has turned into a lively, noisy beehive."

After that, besides the regular Room 2 noises, there were a lot of buzzing sounds, too.

The backdrop looked messy to Billy, like a wall of graffiti from an abandoned building, or something Sal would have done if she'd been let loose with paints and a brush. But Ms. Silver had a different opinion. When the backdrop was finished, she stood with her hands on her hips and studied it. She smiled and nodded. "It's beautiful," she said. Her smile was so wide there were big dents in her cheeks.

Ms. Silver had invitations printed for the big night. She left space on the fronts of the invitations so that the students could decorate them. "Make them personal," she said. "Make them your own."

Billy drew a picture of Poetry Man on his invitation, complete with four arms and his hat. He thought Mama and Papa would like it.

Emma leaned toward Billy and stared intently at his drawing. She made a sour face and said, "Why did you draw an instrument? For your information, we're not having a musical concert."

Billy moved his drawing closer to his chest and tightened his grip on his marker. After months of sitting by her, Billy had learned that the best way to deal with Emma was to

206

ignore her. But in his private thoughts, he said, "For *your* information, mind your own business."

"I'm drawing my grandma on my invitation," said Emma. "She's coming all the way from Minneapolis for the show. I memorized my poem because it makes it more special if you memorize."

Billy gripped his marker even tighter. He wondered if Emma was right. He wondered if memorizing your poem *did* make it more special. He hadn't seriously considered memorizing his poem until now. If he could do it, Mama might be especially happy. And proud. If he could do it, it would be a way to prove how smart he was.

ᕲᐧᕲ

Billy memorized his poem. He didn't tell anyone. It was a secret between him and Poetry Man. It would be a surprise for Mama.

At the final rehearsal for the show, on the stage, with the microphone, Billy thought he should give it a try—he'd recite his poem from memory. But he was so startled and mesmerized by what the microphone did to the sound of his voice when he said the title of his poem that he forgot every word of it. Luckily, he had a copy of it in his hand. After taking a deep breath, he read from his paper in a voice that seemed big enough to fill every inch of the school.

He thought: At least this wasn't the show.

He thought: I still have my chance to do it for real.

He thought: Now that I know what it's like to use a microphone, I can do it perfectly for Mama.

5

Before they left for the show, Billy sneaked to Sal's room to look for the pearl he'd given her months earlier. He knew she kept a shoe box of her favorite things under her bed. He figured that that would be a good place to check first.

He found it. The pearl was there, in the shoe box, among seashells, pebbles, and Sal's new favorite thing—her collection of little erasers in the shapes of animals. He rubbed

the pearl against his shirt and slipped it into his front pants pocket. He needed all the luck he could get. He'd return it after the show.

"Do you have your poem?" Mama asked before they left the house.

Billy held up his copy of the poem. He'd folded it into quarters.

"I hope you know how much I love it," she said. "It's a great poem."

"Thanks," said Billy.

"Papa helped *me* write a poem," said Sal. "Listen—

211

THE YEAR OF BILLY MILLER

Roses are red,

Violets are blue,

Billy's a poet,

And I am, too."

"Sweet," said Mama.

"Aren't we original?" said Papa.

"Ms. Silver wouldn't allow any 'Roses are red' poems," said Billy. "They're too easy," he added with authority.

"Is everyone ready?" asked Papa. He'd filled a backpack with plastic containers of his homemade cookies for the party after the show. He slung the backpack over his shoulder. "Onward," he said.

Sal was holding Raindrop by her tail. Now

she usually took just one Drop Sister with her when she was away from home.

Billy's family met Ned's family at the corner and they walked together.

Billy knew how important the show was because they were having it after dinner on a school night. It felt strange and exciting to be going to school at this time of day.

"Only six more days of school," Ned said gleefully.

"Six more days," said Billy.

"Six more days," Papa echoed, shaking his head. "Where did the year go?"

Billy and Ned swung their arms dramatically, lifted their knees high, and jutted their chins. They marched and chanted

213

through the still, heavy air. "Six more days! Six more days!"

The air in the auditorium was heavy, but it was not still—it was electric. At least, that's the way it felt to Billy. Parents, brothers, sisters, grandparents, aunts, uncles, neighbors, and friends were filling up the room. People were talking and fanning themselves. Little kids were chasing up and down the aisles and climbing on the seats. Eruptions of laughter came and went in waves.

Ms. Silver had saved seats in the front rows for the Room 2 poets and their special guests. Each reserved seat had a student's or a guest's name taped to it. The students and guests would be sitting in the order in which they would appear on stage.

To signal the start of the show, Ms. Silver sounded her gong. Everyone found their places. Billy sat between Mama and Emma's grandmother. Silence descended upon the auditorium like a spell. When the curtain opened, revealing the backdrop, Ms. Silver swept her arm out toward it, and the audience applauded.

"Room Two presents *We Are Family*—" said Ms. Silver, "our celebration of poetry and those we love."

Ms. Silver stood at the corner of the stage. A small microphone was clipped to her dress. The big microphone was at the center of the stage—gleaming and waiting.

"Our first poet will be Grace Cotter," Ms. Silver announced. "Her special guest is her uncle Zack. Next up will be Jamaica Taylor."

Grace and her uncle mounted the three stairs to the stage. As Grace passed in front of her, Ms. Silver handed Grace a copy of her poem. Grace and her uncle walked slowly to the microphone.

Jamaica and her father waited against the wall, at the bottom of the stairs, ready to go.

At first, Grace was too far away from the microphone, but her uncle nudged her closer. Then, she ended up sideways, facing him rather than the audience, as she read her poem. When she finished she was to exit backstage, go through a hallway, and return to her seat. She ran off the stage while the audience clapped.

And so it went. Ms. Silver would announce each poet, state who was up next, and hand a copy of the poem to the poet on the way to the microphone.

Billy had a hard time paying attention to what was happening on the stage. He kept saying the words to his poem in his head. He knew his poem so well he figured he would still be able to say it by heart when he was ninety.

From time to time, Mama looked at Billy and smiled.

Before long, Ms. Silver said, "Our next poet is Emma Sparks. Her grandmother, Judy, is her special guest. Following Emma will be Billy Miller."

Billy and Mama rose and walked along the wall to the corner of the stage. Billy had left his copy of his poem on his seat. He'd folded and unfolded it so many times, it was falling apart. He'd get a new copy from Ms. Silver. Just in case.

Billy watched Emma. She walked up the stairs with such confidence. She lifted her head and turned it away from Ms. Silver when she glided past her on the stage. She didn't take a copy of her poem. And when she recited her poem—slowly, loudly, and with expression—she flapped her hands about like birds as if to say: Look at me. Of course,

I memorized my poem. And I don't need to have a copy of it in case I forget the words, because forgetting the words would be impossible for me. When she finished, she grinned a know-it-all grin and took a deep bow.

After a few long moments of applause, Billy heard Ms. Silver say his name. It was his turn. If Emma can do it, I can do it, he thought as he ascended the stairs to the stage. Ms. Silver smiled at Billy and offered him a copy of his poem, but he smiled back at her, shook his head, and whispered, "I don't need it." He rubbed Sal's pearl in his pocket one last time as he made his way to the middle of the stage. He could sense Mama right behind him.

Billy inched up to the microphone. He looked out at the audience. When he'd practiced with the microphone, only Room 2 kids were watching. Now, there seemed to be an ocean of people watching, stretching from wall to wall and fanning back toward the doors.

A shivery feeling shot through him. It was a good feeling at first. He tried to locate Papa and Sal among the sea of heads, but he couldn't. And then the good feeling turned bad—he had an odd sensation that the world around him was moving in all directions.

His mouth was dry.

His heart was pounding.

Once again, he forgot every word of his

220

poem, including the title—but this time he didn't have a copy of it to read from.

He saw Ms. Silver in the fringes of his vision. She was smiling and nodding, urging him on with her wide eyes.

Should he walk over to her to get a copy of his poem? She seemed about a mile away. And he didn't think he could make his legs move.

What should he do?

The air felt weird all of a sudden. As if it had sprouted wings and was brushing against him. The air was fluttering against his arm.

How could that be?

He turned around and Mama was there

with a copy of his poem, tapping it lightly against his elbow. "Here," she whispered. "You can do it."

And he could.

And he did.

He read his poem into the microphone from beginning to end in a voice that was made so big and loud and wide it seemed to bounce beyond the walls of school, reaching to the world outside, to the moon.

Everyone clapped. He heard Papa whistle, although he still couldn't spot him.

The next thing he knew he was in the hallway behind the stage, enveloped in Mama's arms. On the stage, it was as if he'd been separated from his body, and now he'd

222

caught up with himself. Everything was back to normal.

"You did it!" said Mama. "You did it beautifully."

"But I didn't do it by heart," said Billy.

"It doesn't matter."

"How did you have a copy of my poem?" asked Billy.

"I took it from Ms. Silver when I followed you onto the stage," replied Mama.

A moment passed and then Billy asked, "Did you think that I couldn't do it?"

Without missing a beat, Mama said, "I just wanted a souvenir from this wonderful night."

Whatever the reason, Billy was grateful that Mama had done what she'd done.

They went back to their seats to watch the rest of the show.

After the show, refreshments were served on long tables in the back of the auditorium. Billy had four of Papa's cookies. Ned tried to eat one of each different food item. Everyone was talking about the experience of being on stage.

"Did you hear that incredible screechy sound when I was up there?" asked Ned. "My dad says it's called feedback. I had major feedback," he bragged.

"When I was up there," said Billy, "there were so many people, I couldn't even see my dad."

"All I know," said Emma, "is that I ended up being the only memorizer."

Emma's comment nagged at Billy. He'd already recited his poem from memory in his head two times since the show had ended. He tried to convince himself that it didn't matter. And he told himself that he could recite it for Mama at home.

People were milling about—eating, laughing, chatting—when Ms. Silver's gong sounded. A hush came over the room. Ms. Silver was at the center of the stage, by the microphone.

"Thank you, everyone," said Ms. Silver. "We accomplished a lot this year—not just putting on this marvelous show."

A few people clapped. Mama touched Billy's shoulder. Papa winked at him. Sal made Raindrop dance.

"We studied and learned so much," Ms. Silver continued. "We worked hard." She smiled and raised one hand up near her heart. "Our school year overlapped with the Chinese Year of the Rabbit *and* the Year of the Dragon. But I like to think of this as the Year of Room Two."

Everyone clapped and cheered for a long time. Ms. Silver stepped away from the microphone and waved enthusiastically as she walked to the corner of the stage and down the stairs.

It looked to Billy as if Ms. Silver might cry.

Some of the parents rushed to Ms. Silver to hug her. She slowly made her way to the back of the room by the food. People began eating and laughing and chatting again.

No one seemed to notice as Billy moved quietly toward the stage, weaving through clusters of people. He took the stairs lightly and stepped up to the microphone.

Billy looked out onto the auditorium. No one was staring at him. No one was paying attention. He almost felt alone.

He touched the silver netted top of the microphone and he could tell that the power was off. He swallowed. Before he could change his mind, he began to recite his poem from memory. He felt the first few words catch in his mouth and then they rolled out of him as easy as could be.

He did it quickly, but he did it. When he was finished, he could hear the rush of blood in his ears. He felt light, as if he weighed next to nothing.

He scanned the crowd for Mama, and he saw her instantly. She was right at the foot of the stage. Their eyes connected, and he knew that she'd been watching him. She'd heard him, even without the microphone on. She was smiling and nodding.

Explosions like little volcanoes were going

off inside him. He felt wonderful. Maybe, he'd never felt better.

And then, because he felt so good, and because he could not stop himself, he leaned into the silent microphone and exclaimed in a voice meant just for Mama, "This is the Year of Billy Miller."